ATTRITION

Emilio Iasiello

For information, or to order additional copies,
please contact:

Beacon Publishing Group
P.O. Box 41573 Charleston, S.C. 29423
800.817.8480| beaconpublishinggroup.com

Publisher's catalog available by request.

ISBN-13: 978-1-949472-15-8

ISBN-10: 1-949472-15-8

Published in 2020. Printed in the USA.

First Edition. New York, NY 10001

"My conscience hath a thousand tongues
And every tongue has a tale
And every tale condemns me for a villain."
-William Shakespeare

Emilio Iasiello

Preface

Worcester, Massachusetts
March 17, 1969 – St. Patrick's Day

Night firmly fell over Worcester. For mid-March, the weather was unusually warm. Winters had a way of entrenching themselves deeply into the fabric of New England. But not tonight. Whether it was a warm front that pushed its way in from the west, or St. Patrick himself providing good drinking weather for his day's celebrants, a sweater and a few shots of whiskey were enough to keep the cold away and the party going well into the night.

Loud, drunken singing penetrated the darkness. Inside a dive bar, college kids belted out "The Wild Rover" for the umpteenth time. Their voices slurred, full of slovenly drunken passion that made the lyrics nearly incomprehensible.

Tucked away off Oxford Street, "Murphy's Lounge" was more a large trailer propped up on blocks than an actual bar. Buried at the base of a dead-end street, Murphy's bordered an impassible fence on one side and a fenced-in junkyard on the other.

It catered to locals, blue-collar patrons fond of cheap beer and a place that hadn't completely surrendered to the whims of the affluent students attending the college on the hill. Despite some tensions between the vastly different clienteles,

1

business was still business. As the city continued to decay post-World War II, its manufacturing base folded to less expensive alternatives in other regions. Legal tender from college students was plentiful as long as an establishment didn't mind a couple of snot-nose kids acting out of line from time to time.

The two social classes generally found an uneasy middle ground with one another, and for the most part, stayed with their own groups when inside Murphy's. Murphy himself was a potbellied local who used to be a firefighter but took a settlement after being injured on the job. He bought the establishment as an investment. In his mind, two things were reliable in Worcester – blue collar work ethic kept the city afloat and alcohol consumption kept the working-class folk at their backbreaking jobs.

Murphy was affable and polite to the college crowd, although his interest and favor fell on the young freshmen girls taking advantage of escaping the watchful gaze of parents to venture to the Lounge and try their first beer. Once they left, Murphy would trash talk the students, particularly those that came in with close-cropped haircuts, sports coats and wing-tip shoes. Future bankers or lawyers or whatever their parents molded them to be.

On that cool spring evening, the bar's side door suddenly sprang open, allowing the inebriated cacophony of Irish folk music to escape the capacity-filled ragged bare-bones box. A young woman, no more than eighteen, stumbled outside, barely clinging on to her biology textbook. Dark haired and glassy-eyed, the freshman steadied herself on the porch railing with both hands, before slowly and methodically making her way down the three rotting wooden stairs to the street.

She was in good spirits and in relatively good ambulatory state given the day she had. The textbook she had brought along to glance at for the upcoming test remained unopened the entire day. First, she attended the "Kegs and Eggs" morning party at a house full of seniors on Carol Street. Then there were lunch cocktails at her roommate's sister's apartment on Oxford Circle. A pub crawl soon followed, starting at Shenanigans and concluding at Murphy's. Along the way she drank green beer, ate green eggs, and had a plethora of colored shots – some green, some not – composed of liquors whose names she had never heard of before.

But the piece de resistance – she found some private time to talk with Darren McClone, the sandy-blonde haired boy in her "Intro to English Literature" class. Darren was quiet, attentive, and had the absolute dreamiest pale blue eyes she had ever seen. Boys like Darren didn't come from where she was from – a little town no one heard of in New Hampshire. There, boys tended to be a little less – what was the word her friend had used? Polished. They were accustomed to wearing their jeans three days in a row and had to be reminded to chew with their mouths closed when sitting across from someone, especially a girlfriend.

Hers was the first class to admit women at the college, a fact in which she took substantial pride. Her parents didn't want her to be part of some "social experiment" – her father's words, but she wanted to be part of something from the ground floor. She minded his words about boys and drinking but she knew she was ready for the world outside the tiny hamlet in which she was born and reared.

This is not to say that she disliked her hometown. On the contrary, she saw herself settling back there after she experienced college and spent some time in those places she had always wanted to see – Venice, Paris, even Hollywood. Then she could be content in re-rooting herself to the familiar, finding a good man, and having kids.

She succeeded in making it to the main road without falling. She turned toward her destination. In the distance, the College of Saint Sebastian's gothic structure could be seen atop the hill. A normally long but manageable walk was now complicated by a high blood-alcohol content and too little sleep.

To keep her mind from languishing on the endeavor before her, the girl thought about her college career thus far. Almost eight months in, she had survived the trials and tribulations that confronted freshmen ill-equipped to handle the transition to college. Many of her friends had found freedom too liberating, favoring drinking and all-night procrastination over homework and studying. She, on the other hand, found managing classes and the maze of social life relatively easy. As much as she didn't want to admit, most of that credit had to go to her parents. Born to parents who defined the workday as "day-break to back-break" made one do more with less, assume more responsibility without recompense, and not complain at every injustice because there was invariably someone who had it worse.

She made it to the corner, deciding to take a break. She sat with her textbook on the stoop next to the gas station to rest her legs and gain her bearings. She wasn't sure what time it was, only that it was late, and she was looking forward to her bed with its two large pillows and plush duck feather comforter.

At the gas pumps, a man removed the gas cap to his brown car and inserted a nozzle. He looked in his forties, with five days of beard on his face and greasy hair. Off coordination and a slight wobble in his movements suggested that he was in between parties, or at least rounds of booze.

He looked up and noticed her looking at him. She quickly averted her eyes, flushing with embarrassment.

The man smiled, wondering if his Irish blood would prove lucky on the luckiest day of the year.

"Where you headed to?" he asked her. His voice didn't slur but tilted on the edge of acceptability.

The young woman looked over at him. He smiled at her. It was too big, too aggressive, for someone just trying to be friendly.

"Going back to my dorm," she said. She silently cursed herself out for providing that information. She blamed the last two shots on her inability to process information quickly.

The man opened the driver's door and removed two cans of beer from inside. He walked over to her with one in his hand.

"How about a drink?" he offered.

"No thanks."

"Come on. Don't tell me you don't drink. I know you drink. You look like you had a few yourself tonight. Hell, I'm just catching up."

He held the beer out to her again. She looked at the can of Schlitz and took it. She pulled the tab and took a sip. It was warm.

"I'm looking for a party," he said. "You know of any parties going on?"

She shook her head.

"You'd think there'd be a handful tonight. You sure none of your friends don't have a kegger somewheres? Someplace hush-hush or something like that?"

"No, I'm just a freshman."

"Well, that's okay, sweetheart. We can make our own party. I got two six packs in the truck."

"Thanks, but I should be going back. I've got school tomorrow."

"Sure you do, and I got work. But you know what? It's St. Paddy's. I'll let you in on a little secret. No one's going to make it into work, and if I know college kids, you ain't going to make it to class."

Maybe it was the casual way he said it. Maybe it was his tone. Either way, she didn't like it. She set aside the can of beer.

"I have to go. Thanks for the beer."

"You didn't finish it. That's alcohol abuse."

He grabbed the beer. He lifted it to his mouth. Like a serpent, his tongue darted quickly out, licking the part of the rim where she put her mouth.

"Oh, honey, you are sweet."

Repulsed, she turned in the direction of her dorm. The man's hand bolted out, grabbing her arm.

"Come on, I'm just playing with you."

"Let go, please. You're hurting my arm."

"I'm just trying to be friendly. I got laid off today."

"You just said you had to go to work tomorrow."

The man's face darkened. He didn't like the smart-aleck mouth on this girl.

"I don't feel like getting shunned by a tight-twatted college girl."

She froze at the malevolence of the man's tone. She was too scared to move and stared at him like a deer in the increasing aperture of approaching headlights.

"Leave her alone."

She didn't see the person behind the voice. It came from somewhere behind the man. Based on tone and depth, it belonged to a college-age man. He sounded young, but his voice brooked no arguments.

The local turned in the direction of the voice.

"And what are you going to do about it?"

"Me? Nothing. Me and my three friends? Well, we may just do something."

She didn't feel well. She moved away from the group and fumbled down the street. She needed a safe place to clear her head and get rooted. She spotted the cemetery at the base of the hill and knew there was a shortcut there that would get her off the main road and closer to her dormitory.

The cemetery was an old Jesuit graveyard attached to Saint Sebastian's. There was a time that the institution had only Jesuit teachers. But that changed over the years and now there were only a handful on campus teaching English, political science, and religious studies. When they died, they were buried in this little sanctuary. The cemetery held custody of the bodies of eighty Jesuits, all former teachers. The last priest to be interned was ten years ago. Now the cemetery was more ceremonial, a time capsule of headstones with dates going back as far as the 1800s. This was a place where kids drank, or made out, or just went to be by themselves.

She took a seat on a large headstone that read "Featherstone". She hoped that the priest's spirit didn't mind. Her head was swimming and she needed the quiet and the air to help shake the haze free from her head. She was too focused on clearing that mass of confusion that she did not notice the headlights of the car along the road. The car passed by, then stopped, and slowly backed up, finally idling along the side of the street.

The young woman stood and looked for the path that led up the hill to the school. She couldn't immediately find it and started over to the edge of the tree line that served as a boundary where there wasn't a wrought-iron gate.

Something unnerved her. She stopped, listening for the unfamiliar. Looking around, twisted shadows taunted her sensibilities.

She inhaled deeply, then held it. She shut her eyes, listening intently.

What was that – a rustle?

She strained to focus her vision. Nothing showed itself. There was a slight wind. But, so what?

She noticed the car across the street. A door was left open. Was she alone?

"Hello?" she called out to the shadows surrounding her.

Spooked and desperate to get home, she failed to see the headstone before her knee met it, sending her crashing face-forward to the ground. Her shriek resembled the sound an animal made when the snare's wire trapped its leg. More surprise then pain.

The noises were more distinct now. She frantically looked around. Fear sharpened her senses, but alcohol blurred their effectiveness. It didn't matter. She heard him – or them – or whoever or whatever was there.

"Go away!" she screamed.

Her blood ran cold when she heard someone laugh in response to her request.

She got up and sprinted forward. She didn't make it.

Someone's arms grabbed her from behind and threw her on the ground. She landed hard, expelling the breath she had been holding as her textbook went flying. She fought to draw air into her lungs. She wanted to breathe again. She didn't pay attention to the figure above her. She tried to speak but nothing came out.

The intention was clear.

A hand found her breast and squeezed. Another wrestled to get under her dress.

"No-no-no-no-no…"

She flailed, hitting a shoulder, but there was little effect. Her feeble strikes thumped dully against the more powerful figure.

The fingers were invasive and cold. She was aware of the hot tears streaming down her face and the digits eager to find their way between her legs.

She summoned her strength and bolted upright. Her head collided into her attacker's chin. She saw stars, but the smack of bone against bone was enough. Her unseen attacker swore and broke contact with her.

She scrambled to her feet. In the street, a pack of drunken students walked by. They were loud and laughing. Drunk and happy and safe.

She tried to scream but nothing came out.

A silhouette obstructed her view.

"Get back here, bitch!"

Fight or flight. Panicked, she took off in the other direction. The frenzied pace prevented her from finding proper footing.

She tripped over a marker. Stumbling to regain balance, she careened away, walloping her head against a headstone shaped like a Fleury Cross.

Eyes open, she gasped for breath as the blood pooled around her and down her face blurring her vision.

She could barely make out the silhouette of a figure standing over here staring down into the once bright eyes whose light was fading away.

Chapter 1

Neal Farnsworth stood by the window of his doctor's office. Outside, the late afternoon sky darkened steadily like a piece of bruised fruit. He watched the steady swell of traffic, cars jockeying to get an edge on the others for the return commute to their suburban homes.

At sixty-one years old, Farnsworth's body had held up well since his college days. A combination of exercise and eating the right foods had set him on a healthy path for the past ten years, all thanks to his wife's polite but firm insistence. Unfortunately, she didn't see his full transformation, having passed away due to complications brought on by breast cancer, a diagnosis that ran in her family. Entering his golden years, Farnsworth found himself alone, and since they had no offspring, it would have been easy to slip into full-on self-pitying debauchery. But he didn't. He loved his wife and wanted to follow through on his promise to take care of himself, to eat better, to exercise better, to be better. A better person in body and mind.

And now he was waiting for his doctor to tell him the test results.

Farnsworth turned from the window and sat on the chair across from his doctor's desk. It was messy with folders and papers strewn about in a haphazard professionalism. He crossed his legs, adjusting the crease in his pant lines so they were just right. He noticed the scar on his wrist and ran a thumb over the raised pucker. Sometimes he forgot it was there, a reminder of his wilder days in college when he and his friends took things to excess. He started to think about them when the door opened, and Bill Pearlstone walked inside. Three years older than Farnsworth, Dr. Pearlstone was both his and his wife's primary physician. The doctor held a file in his hands. His face was solemn.

"Gee Bill, when you said you'd be right back, I thought you meant sometime today," Farnsworth said. He tried to make his voice sound light and carefree, but the words hung heavy in the air.

Dr. Pearlstone didn't immediately reply. Instead, he pulled up a chair next to his patient and friend. He coughed once and rubbed a palm against his thigh. He didn't – couldn't – make immediate eye contact.

A sinking feeling settled in Farnsworth's stomach.

"Why do I feel like I'm in trouble with the principal here, Bill?"

Dr. Pearlstone cleared his voice.

"Goddammit, Neal, how can you make a joke out of everything?"

"I'm not making a joke. I'm waiting for my doctor to speak to me."

"I know. I'm sorry," Pearlstone sighed. He took his time and collected his thoughts. "You know I've been practicing medicine for nearly forty years?"

"And it never gets easier," Farnsworth said.

The doctor looked at his friend. He half-smiled. There was no need to sugar coat things. His patient was a billionaire. He had made tough decisions, heard tough news, and still found a way to maneuver through pitfalls to rise to the top. And maybe that's what made this difficult. Pearlstone could anticipate the reactions of his patients to bad news and could prepare himself for it. With Neal, it was different. He was already one step ahead and prepared for the one after.

"Give it to me straight, Bill."

"Do I have to? You already know the answer."

The doctor surrendered the file to his friend. Now, it was his turn to stand and take refuge by the window. He was less concerned about what he saw and more about what he heard from his patient.

Farnsworth's face remained expressionless. He flipped through every page, his eyes scanning through various images and pages of notes that read more like Greek than English. But he didn't have to understand the words and what they meant. As Pearlstone thought, he already knew the answer, and was almost ashamed that he had broached the subject in the first place.

Farnsworth set the folder on the desk. Now he needed facts. Even death required a business plan that had to be drafted, developed, and implemented.

"What am I looking at?"

Pearlstone turned back to his friend.

"Eight to twelve months, tops. Once it settles in, you'll deteriorate quickly. If you have any affairs that you need to take care of, sooner is better than later."

Farnsworth stood. He had to show the doctor that he was still in control, that his body hadn't given out yet.

And then he did the most unexpected thing – he laughed. It started out as a sharp bark but grew loud and uncontrollable until tears glistened his eyes.

"You okay, Neal? You want me to write a prescription?"

"Kale," Farnsworth said.

"Kale?"

"Deborah wanted me to eat more kale before she died. She said it would keep me healthy. I should have stuck with Big Macs."

*****

Turnberry Tower was the tallest residential building in downtown Boston. Sculpted out of glass and steel, it seemed more art than residence, more aesthetic than function. It overlooked the Charles River and was a stone's throw from the Massachusetts Institute of Technology. Many of the

He didn't usually allow himself moments to miss Deborah, but now was a rare occasion. He picked up the photograph of them both and ran an index finger over his wife's face.

"What would you have me do?" he asked her. "You always let me know when I was steering off course. Help me get back there."

He waited for a few moments but there was no response, not that he expected there to be one. He smiled and set the photograph back down.

Farnsworth ambled over to his safe in the study. For the next two hours, he compiled all necessary documents and papers that he would need for the next day. When he was finished, he had filled two banker's boxes. The next hours were spent making phone calls and lining up appointments for the next day. There was minor pushback, but as was customary, everyone fell in line with his wishes. It was close to eleven o'clock when he collapsed in the large leather wing-backed study chair.

He closed his eyes to rest them for a few minutes before continuing to get things together for tomorrow's meetings. But for a man accustomed to getting his own way, nature won this round and Farnsworth's breath found a steady rhythm as the dying man finally surrendered to sleep.

*****

Meetings started a little before eight in the morning and did not end until seven that evening.

There was a seemingly never-ending onslaught of attorneys, the board, PowerPoint presentations, recommendations on C-Suite positions, and an outlined strategy of the company's direction for the next ten years.

The news was a shock. Questions were asked, most of them deflected by Farnsworth simply telling them that the time had come to leave the company in younger capable hands and to pursue other interests. Although no one protested, those whom had worked with Farnsworth sensed a deeper underlying motive lurking beneath the surface. But they all knew better than to inquire further. By knowing the man, they knew when to stop heading down a forbidden path of questioning their leader's judgment.

Farnsworth politely turned down three lunch offers and a going-away post-work happy hour. He cited his numerous other responsibilities and commitments that needed his attention over the course of the week to ensure a smooth transition. The final stop in the afternoon was to his personal attorney, Marty Quinlan, an old friend of his from college who was a senior when Farnsworth was a sophomore.

After signing a ream of documents that took close to an hour, both men sat in Marty's plush office. Marty retrieved a bottle of single malt scotch and two glasses from the wet bar, setting them down on his desk.

"So, do I get to ask?"

"No regrets," Marty said. "You go on to your Maker with a clean conscience. You'd be surprised how many people don't. My two cents for what it's worth."

A look crossed Farnsworth face. It was the moment of unexpected realization, when the face registers an involuntary reaction somewhere between terror and inspiration.

"Tie up loose ends," he repeated. "That's not a bad idea."

Farnsworth stood up and stretched a hand to him.

"Thanks, Marty," he said.

"What's your hurry?"

"Clock's ticking, so to speak."

"Don't hesitate, Neal. Whatever you need. I'm here."

"You sure about that?"

"That's what I do. And I am your friend. I outstretch my hand to shake, not take."

Farnsworth laughed.

"You should put that on your letterhead."

Marty walked Farnsworth to the door. He clasped his client-friend on the shoulder to reiterate his pledge.

"I'm serious," he said again. "Anything."

"I know," Farnsworth said.

*****

At the bar in the sunk-in living room, Farnsworth poured himself three fingers worth of Pappy Van Winkle's 23-year old Family Reserve. The day ran longer than planned and it took more of a toll on his body than he had expected. Behind him, Bach's Fugue in G-Minor's haunting melody cried from a vintage Hudson turntable. The organ music seemed fitting now that he had received his news, digested it, and accepted it. Rather than depressing, the somber tone and voice of the music seemed one appropriate and respectful of the situation.

Farnsworth stood in front of a wall lined with long shelves that show-cased an array of games – board games, card games, role-playing games, computer games, and video games. The same company logo emblazoned across every game box – Farnsworth Enterprises. What initially started out as a whim ultimately became the source of his wealth and prosperity. While many of his college classmates moved onto careers in law and medicine, Farnsworth took his English degree and his unborrowed vision and created his first game – *To Drop a Dime* – a board game that capitalized on America's infatuation with the Italian Mafia, and the success of Coppola's *The Godfather*. It took off and Farnsworth had never looked back. He always enjoyed the principle behind games – the purpose was already preconditioned – enjoyment – but a good game designer was empathetic and always understood what was going on inside a player's head.

And Farnsworth knew nothing if he didn't know people – how they thought, how they would act, how they would respond to variables.

"So much done, so much to do," he mused to himself.

He walked over to the box that he had dug out of one of his many closets. Inside was memorabilia from college – a scarf of the school's colors, a program from senior year's homecoming day football game, random mugs, and the one item he wanted to see – his graduation yearbook.

Farnsworth thumbed through the pages of the senior class, coursing over faces that were dimly familiar and names in some cases that he had never even heard of. One by one he stopped at the faces of his three closest friends and roommates in college: Bernard "Bernie" Michaels; Theodore "Teddy" Strickler; and Ethan Chance. Despite being all in their early twenties, their faces were remarkably boyish, cleanly shaven and haircuts that were "high and tight", the popular style at the primarily conservative Jesuit institution.

Marty had a point. These were his friends. His best friends at one time. Sure, maybe their lives had taken a wrong turn and maybe they had each asked for a helping hand at one point after college. What of it? There were other things too – he could never forget those – but now that his stopwatch on earth was ticking off his remaining time, shouldn't that be water under the bridge?

Deborah wouldn't agree. She was much too practical for that. Water under a bridge was a stream; events that form and shape people's lives were a different thing altogether.

Farnsworth set down the yearbook and headed over to an architect's table near the window. Below it was a notebook in which he penned ideas for new games. He set it on the table, flipping through the pages until he found the section he was looking for. His eyes quickly scanned the written notes. He spent the next hour transcribing his brainstorming scribbling into a more organized outline. He jotted down words like "Setting" and "Character" and "Costume" and "Mystery." He pulled out a map of the United States and ran a finger along the New England states, marking down Connecticut, Massachusetts, New Hampshire, Vermont, and Maine. For the first time since he was delivered the news, Farnsworth smiled – not wryly or sarcastically, but one born out of the act of the satisfaction of his effort.

Through the floor-to-ceiling windows, Farnsworth watched the sun creep over the horizon. He found his cell phone and dialed a number.

"Marty, it's Neal. I need to make some adjustments to my will. And I'm going to need a hand getting some permits. And I need to be your only client until…well, you understand. Thanks."

Farnsworth hung up the phone. Despite all his accomplishments, there was still one more thing to do. And knowing that gave him a reinvigorated purpose. He couldn't die yet. Not just yet.

Chapter Two

Three Months Later

The black cherry Dodge Shadow was parked next to an old Iroc Z on a grassy inlet off the main road. Shielded by a canopy of trees and overgrown brush, the location was used by the local police as a speed trap when monthly quotas needed to be fulfilled. In the mornings, it was a nondescript location to toss empty beer bottles, urinate, or any other purpose that required concealment from the public eye.

The Dodge was filthy and in need of a desperate cleaning. A series of small dents dimpled the car's back flank and a broken front bumper looked more like a missing tooth in an old, craggy mouth. A first glance intimated that someone set the car out to pasture, abandoning it to die with dignity along the side of the road. But despite its ragged condition, the vehicle showed signs of life, shaking ever-so-slightly in a side-to-side rocking motion, a gesture fitting its lone bumper sticker – *if this car's a rockin', don't come a-knockin."*

Inside the Dodge, heavy panting drowned out the song on the radio. A woman's hand reached for the volume and turned it up.

"I love this fucking song," she said. Journey's "Don't' Stop Believing" pumped through the speakers.

Michaels sat in the front seat reclined back as far as it could go. His pants were down around his ankles and his hands rested on either thigh of the woman straddling him. At sixty years of age, Michaels' face did not display enjoyment as much as a world-weary fatigue and self-loathing. His eyes looked past the bucking bleached blonde on top of him to the cracked windshield. The crack had spider-webbed since he first noticed it two days ago. At five hundred bucks a pop, he wondered how long he could drive with it before a cop pulled him over and issued him a ticket.

"Oh God, oh God, oh God, oh God..." Lorraine cried out. She was a travel agent in town. He had met her at Shenanigans during a boy's night out. In her mid-forties, she wasn't much of a looker, but who was he to complain? She was about as much of a raving beauty as he was. But they had made eyes at one another, until finally she and her three friends joined he and his buddies. What started out as flirting over beers gradually escalated into sharing a plate of mozzarella sticks, and ultimately a blow job and a bump or two of coke in the back-parking lot.

Lorraine was really working it. He gave her a lot of credit. There was no inside voice with Lorraine. She did everything full-on and without care or concern of any other interest or variable that might be in the vicinity. She wasn't getting any younger, she had told him that the third time they hooked up. With this self-realization came a "the plane is crashing" mentality. She was committed to getting the most out of everything – quantity, not quality, being the most important element – anything to hold onto this side of forty.

"Cum baby, cum baby, cum baby…" she said over and over as she hit her rhythm, throwing her head back and letting out a scream that made Michaels shut his eyes and wish he was any other place but there.

*****

In the rear-view mirror, Michaels watched Lorraine climb back into her Iroc Z and pull out of their little hide-away. He judged himself for a few seconds. For a man who just had sex, he neither looked satisfied nor content. If anything, self-loathing was his status quo most days, coupled with a bit of verbal self-flagellation and self-mockery.

Classic hard rock cassette tapes littered the floor of the front seat. Michaels reached down, picking through the cassettes until he found what he was looking for. He inserted it into the player before reaching into the console for a nearly-empty pint of whiskey.

He screwed the cap open, taking a big mouthful, swishing the whiskey around his mouth.

Lorraine always chewed bright pink bubble gum and kissing her was like licking a spoon clean of confection sugar. He spit the whiskey out the window before finishing the rest of the pint. Then that too went out the window.

He sighed heavily. His eyes found his reflection again in the rear-view mirror.

"Way to live above yourself, Bern'," he said.

He looked over at the passenger's seat and grabbed the envelope on it. He received it in the mail two days ago and did not know what to make of it. His old college buddy, Neal Farnsworth, the cocky kid he used to do bong hits with before going to school dances, a guy who made a fortune making games – *games of all things* – sent him an invitation for a weekend get-away.

A weekend get-away. What the hell was that all about? The last time he spoke to Farnsworth was ten or fifteen years ago when he asked his old roommie for a favor, one that Farnsworth emphatically turned down.

Farnsworth was such an asshole. To be honest, he was an asshole in college too, but at least then he was *his* asshole friend, which seemed to make it alright. Farnsworth was smart but enjoyed being a smart aleck more. He was the type that used his intellect as a precision weapon, cutting down people, embarrassing them in front of crowds, the bigger the better. But the thing with Farnsworth was that he was an equal opportunity jackass. Being his friend didn't make you immune from his sardonic attacks. Michaels was frequently the butt of jokes that teared down his pot smoking, his weight, his dick size. Farnworth had the knack of finding that little insecurity you tried to hide, and like a scab, kept picking at it, reserving the big rip-away when the audience was largest and most receptive.

Still, he was the most successful out of their group of friends. Teddy Strickler was a doctor, and Ethan Chance was in the movies or something, but none of them could touch the heights Farnsworth had achieved by selling games.

Games.

Michaels groaned as he removed the card from the envelope. On it, one word in dark blue capital letters ran along the border of the invitation:

WEEK END WEEK END WEEK END WEEK
END WEEK END…

And in the center of the card in bright red letters:

YOU ARE INVITED

Even the invitation seemed more like a command than a request. Farnsworth always got what he wanted. If you refused or tried to resist, he'd systematically break you down until you came to him with your hat in your hand in penance.

A long weekend with Farnsworth to play a new game he was designing.

Games. God, Michaels couldn't get over it.

Still, maybe this was another chance to get some investment money. Not a handout, but an investment – it was a fine difference from the first time he went to him those many years ago but a difference, nonetheless. Maybe if he went to the little reunion and got Farnsworth alone, he could pitch his idea for the new venture. He wasn't the same burnout as he was in college. He was married. He had a family. It wasn't about joyriding through life, it was about financial security for his family.

He was being an adult.

Michaels dug into his shirt pocket for a travel size bottle of mouthwash. He looked at his watch. It was time to get home.

*****

"A murder mystery? You can't be serious," Suzy said unloading clothes from the washing machine and moving them to the dryer. They had been married for twenty-three years, and had three kids, two girls and one boy. Michaels stood in the hallway watching his wife bend down. She was a good mother, but the sexual spark had long since extinguished. The ass he used to love had expanded with age. He immediately scolded himself for the thought. It wasn't like his stomach was flat or his pecs enormous.

"Farnsworth's company is working on some new game. There's a lot of buzz around it," he lied. He didn't know if there was a buzz or not, but he felt compelled to create the illusion of importance if there was none immediately recognizable.

Suzy slammed the door shut and set the dryer. She opened the cabinet above, removing a pack of cigarettes and lighting one.

"Sounds like an excuse for grown men to act like college boys again."

"Jesus Christ, Suz', we're all in our sixties. I don't think any of us could be a 'college boy' again. Where are the kids?"

"Out. Don't worry. I don't smoke in front of them."

"I know, I know."

She gave him a look, then offered him the butt. He took it, dragging off it.

"I'm going," he said, passing the smoke back. "I have to."

"I figured you weren't asking for permission."

"What's that supposed to mean?"

"It means whatever you want it to mean." She could see the hurt in his eyes and softened. "So, what's this game anyway?"

"Some kind of murder mystery."

Suzy made a face. "What's so special about that?"

"I guess I'll find out. The guy's worth a kajillion dollars. I think he knows what he's doing. If he thinks murder mysteries are a thing, that works for me."

Michaels walked to the spare room where he kept his clothes. Since they had been having problems, he thought it was better to move his stuff to another room so there would be less opportunities for confrontation.

She followed him inside the room, leaning against the doorframe as he rummaged bureau drawers. He referred to a small card in his hand.

"What's that?" she asked him.

"We're supposed to come in character. Have you seen my denim jacket?"

"In the back of the closet. Left side. What character are you supposed to be?"

"You tell me."

Michaels found the denim jacket and tossed it on the floor. He threw a black concert t-shirt and raggedy torn jeans alongside it.

"A roadie?" she asked.

"A thief."

She walked over to one of the drawers and pulled out a gray hoodie.

"Now you look like a thief," she said.

"Thanks," he said.

She looked at the Wild Turkey poster on the wall.

"No drinking. Promise me."

"Not even a drop of maraschino cherry juice," he said, trying to make a joke.

"I'm serious, Bernie. You've been clean for six months. Don't ruin that. I don't have a lot to be proud of when it comes to you."

He could tell she was upset. "Look, I know what you think of Farnsworth. I'm on board, trust me. But I have to take this chance. If I can get some private time, talk to him, then maybe, maybe... You know?"

"He didn't give you the money the first time you asked him, Bern. What do you think will change now?"

"How many times are you going to crucify me for Katelynn?"

He tried to sound angry, but his voice was full of guilt.

"I didn't mention our daughter, Bernie. You said so yourself – Farnsworth only likes tormenting those who want something from him. Why do you want to set yourself up again for that? He just rubs your nose in his money. He always has."

"If he invests, it won't matter, will it?"

"What if he doesn't? Is Melissa's college fund a part of the equation like Katelynn's was?"

The remark struck home and struck deep.

"Thanks for the vote of confidence."

Michaels grabbed a suitcase and angrily crammed some clothes inside. He took it and pushed past her and went down the hall toward the kitchen.

He grabbed a pack of Twinkies and shoved them into his coat. Suzy appeared moments later, holding something behind her back.

"You don't even do a good job hiding it from me anymore."

"Oh yeah? What's that?"

She held up a white button-down shirt. On the collar was the unmistakable red smear of lipstick.

"Every night there's lipstick on your collar, and in the morning, I wash it away."

She tossed the shirt on the floor.

"I won't take it any more you son-of-a-bitch. I won't."

Michaels was about to say something but thought better of it. There was no comeback. Not for that.

He went out the door without looking back. He couldn't. As of this moment, there was only what lay ahead.

******

Outside a contemporary luxury house in a gated community, two movers carried a sofa to the back of a white moving truck. Close behind them, another duo struggled with a mahogany armoire. One pointed at the Mercedes Benz parked in the driveway with the license plate that read: DR BONE. Someone made a joke in Spanish, and all the movers laughed.

Inside the house, more men in mocha-colored overalls moved with the purpose of worker ants picking up various items and checking them against a master list on a clipboard.

In his home office off the foyer, Theodore Strickler watched as his valuables were unceremoniously removed from his house one by one. The office had been already been stripped of most of its expensive furniture. Only a folding chair and desk remained at which Strickler sat talking on his phone.

"Dr. Strickler? Are you still there?"

Strickler looked at his mobile. His assistant was on speaker.

"Yes, Mina. Sorry. The movers are here."

"Oh, that's right. I'm sorry."

"It's not your problem," he said. "You didn't divorce me."

Strickler's wife –former wife – had that pleasure. The divorce was in large part due to his poor financial planning and investments in a series of risky pharmaceutical start-ups. Back-to-back failures, one sophisticated Ponzi scheme, and an increasing Fentanyl addiction all contributed to the emptying of Stricker's bank accounts. The final straw was a malpractice suit due to a botched surgery largely the result of Strickler being under the influence of the powerful opiate. His wife had it and took appropriate action to preserve what was left of her family's holdings. Getting back on his feet required relocation and startup money. The first was easy, the second was not.

That was until he received Farnsworth's invitation. It was a blast from the past, and Strickler rarely thought about the past and hardly ever about his college days. He thought of college the way people thought of a vacation. It was momentary, pleasurable in some instances, but ultimately a minor step in a sequential progression that took him to medical school, residency, permanent placement, and then private practice. College was nothing more to him than distant memories irrelevant to his current existence.

At least, it was until now.

"I'll be away for a few days, Mina. You won't be able to reach me."

"What about Mrs. Anderson?"

She was one of his few remaining regular patients. That alone should have convinced him to reject the trip. But loyalty wasn't a prized virtue to him. It made people weak. It made them make poor decisions.

"Refer her to Dr. Glazer. Refer the rest of my patients to Dr. Glazer."

There was a noticeable pause on the other end.

"And if Sarah calls?"

Strickler's impassive face grew dark. He fought to control the bile building up.

"Tell that bitch the bank will wire her money the first of the month, every month. "

An awkward pause.

"I meant your daughter, sir."

The words hit Strickler like a bucket-full of cold water. He didn't know what to say, what he could say, so he pressed on.

"Any word from the bank regarding the loan?"

"Mr. Davenport called," Mina said, then stopped abruptly.

"And?"

"I'm sorry, Doctor."

Strickler sat back in the chair. He rubbed his face with his hands. The final nail struck; the coffin lid was now sealed.

"I'm sure something will turn up," she said, trying to sound upbeat.

Picking up the invitation from the pile of bills on his desk, Strickler saw it as a ticket out of his predicament. He never really liked Farnsworth, but in his defense, no one really liked Farnsworth. He was an annoying mosquito that buzzed your ear that you could never quite get rid of. Deep down, Strickler understood that he was jealous of Farnsworth. He was just a bit more handsome, came from a better family, and had just a bit more money than Strickler. Worse, he was a bully. Not necessarily in the physical sense, but verbally and emotionally. Strickler's backbone would disappear when Farnsworth insulted him. And recognizing this weakness made Strickler more susceptible to Farnsworth's manipulation and Farnsworth knew it.

But he was rich. Filthy rich. What was a million dollars to Farnsworth? Yes, he turned down Strickler when he made the jump to private practice, but that was so many years ago. He was older now, and all things considered, much more accomplished than the money-driven individual looking for a few bucks to set up his own operation. The key to getting Farnsworth's money was not asking for it directly. No, Farnsworth would just toy with him then. It had to be calculated and deliberate like good business opportunities were. Yes, he was going to Farnsworth's weekend party, but with a specific goal in mind.

"Something already has," he said. Strickler removed the invitation and a smaller envelope with the words – YOUR CHARACTER. He opened it, read what was written. "Mina, you go clubbing and all of that. Where does someone get a sharkskin jacket?"

******

The Sleepy Hollow Inn was a no-star motel ninety miles from the nearest major metropolis. The Inn had two things going for it – it charged twenty bucks for an overnight stay, or if there was no need to spend the night, management provided flexible and affordable hourly rates. The motel was laid out in a classic "L" formation that bordered a parking lot devoid of any designated space markers. Two ice machines and two soda vending machines were strategically posted at the ends of the "L."

Clientele of the Sleepy Hollow generally consisted of travelers moving from point A to point B. Only a rare few ever stayed more than one night. There wasn't any reason to. The pool had long since been drained and shut down and the sparse amenities and lack of culinary options that didn't require a twenty-minute drive made the Sleepy Hollow an establishment most wanted to avoid.

Independent film makers appreciated the Inn's ragged economy, particularly those that shot their "films" directly on video. Room 12-A was the location of choice, as it was positioned at the elbow of the motel and provided more room for the camera and soundmen to work. Ball Busting Productions rented that room so often that they could have had a preferred customer card.

Inside 12-A, the bare-bones crew set up a series of shots. The three actors stood to the side wearing robes. The blonde smoked a cigarette while the redhead filed her nails. The man did a find-a-word puzzle. Downtime was common on any set, whether you were shooting porn or *Lawrence of Arabia*. The director took the sound man to the side and pointed where he should position the microphones. A makeshift hospitality table was set up on the bureau full of Hostess cupcakes and bottled water. Ball Busting Productions was nothing if it not classy.

Attrition

Ethan Chance sat in a beat-up Chevrolet in the parking lot. He typed on a laptop, pausing every so often to take a drag off a cigarette. In his early sixties, Chance was trim, his boyish good looks aging well and keeping his face relatively wrinkle-free. Chance sat back in the front seat, reading over what he just typed. *The Sorrow Man* – his first novel – was almost complete. It was a fictionalized autobiography of his attempts to make it big in the movie industry as a writer/producer, who suffered insurmountable setbacks, but redeemed himself in the end. The story tracked close to his own life story, save for the ending. He hadn't found his way to redemption, at least not yet. He was still banging out thirty scripts a month for Ball Busting Productions, not a terribly difficult job considering they only consisted of about twenty pages for a thirty-minute shoot.

He looked at the invitation he had received from his college friend Farnsworth. He thought it was a joke at first; he hadn't spoken to Farnsworth in twenty years, when his old roommate turned down his plea for some financial help to get him set up in Hollywood. His parents had just passed away, and Chance was at a cross in his career. He always wanted to be in the movie industry, and he thought this would be his best opportunity. But he was too old to wait tables and his professional experience up until then had been in advertising, a job that he never quite excelled at, and whose talents weren't in any demand.

He didn't think asking his old friend for a loan was crossing any line. Who better than an old friend and roommate to lend a helping hand? Chance should have known better. He more so than anyone else knew of Farnsworth's penchant for public ridicule and humiliation. While he never openly outed Chance, he certainly dropped enough hints about his proclivities toward the same sex. The Catholic college was fiercely conservative and while there was a small gay undercurrent, it was never alluded to or acknowledged. It was a secret that Farnsworth wielded over him like his own personal sword of Damocles.

Chance was so engrossed in fine-tuning his writing that he neglected to notice the director, Tom, exit the room in fit of agitation. He scanned the parking lot until he saw Chance in his car and stormed over to him. He shoved some pages in through the car window.

"What the hell is this bullshit?" Tom said.

The anger broke Chance from his creative focus.

"What's the matter, Tom?" he asked.

Tom opened the door of the car. He may have been twenty years his junior, but Chance still obediently got out.

"Look," Tom said. "I get your artistic angle. I do. It's cute. But I'm not shooting the next *Citizen*

Kane unless it features a strap-on double penetration scene with an actual cane, got it?"

Chance had heard Tom's complaints before. It was true that he tried to give these scripts a bit more punch, better dialogue, the slightest hint of a backstory. He didn't see the big deal. He doubted that providing character motivation would really obstruct the audience from jerking off.

"What are you doing, anyway?" Tom said, gesturing to his laptop in the car.

"My novel, Tom. You said when it was done you'd send it to your father-in-law's publishing house. Well, it's almost done."

"Now's not really a good time, Ethan. Lots of things going on. We need five movies in the can by the end of the month and we're behind schedule."

"It's never a good time, Tom. You owe me this. You *owe* me…"

Maybe it was the tone of his voice or the desperation behind it. Either way, it irritated Tom to no end. He grabbed Chance by the shirt and slammed him hard against the car. Chance's fear excited Tom, and he felt the younger man's erection press into his leg. Tom got his breathing under control and he slowly softened his demeanor and straightened out Chance's shirt.

"Let's keep our eyes on the prize. We're going to finish up our orders, then I swear, I'll personally bring your novel to my father-in-law with my total support, okay?"

This didn't seem to placate Chance. Tom caressed his face lightly.

"Trust me, Ethan. His press publishes talent, and those fingers of yours are very, very talented, just like your mouth…"

He forced a kiss on Chance's mouth. He could only stand there accepting it. He closed his eyes to block it out as Tom's hands squeezed him all over.

Tom ended the kiss and brought Chance's hand to his lips.

"How come you haven't been around the house lately?"

Chance looked away.

"I've been busy. The novel and all."

Tom's finger traced the line of scar across Chance's wrist.

"Maybe you shouldn't be so busy all the time. Maybe you should stop by tonight. Maybe that's what your novel needs."

Chance swallowed hard.

"I can't. I'm going away for a few days."

"Should I be jealous?"

"College friends. A reunion of sorts."

"If you want my help I'll expect to see you at my door first thing when you get back. Is that clear, Ethan?"

"Crystal."

"And if you're getting second thoughts, there aren't too many sixty-year-old cock-sucking would-be novelists trying to publish their first book, right?"

Chance nods. With that, Tom broke into the most affable smile.

"Good. Let's get back to work."

A grimace fastened to his mouth as Chance watched Tom go back inside. His hand shook a bit. He knew that Tom wasn't going to help him. He had done things – horrible things – with that man, for that man, only to be kept at arm's length, drawn in when his sexual sadism needed to be satiated.

Looking at the invitation on the front seat of the car, Chance knew Farnsworth was his last and best chance to break this cycle. He was certain he could convince Farnsworth to help him get his book in the right hands if he could get him to read it.

He decided to send him the book and then they could discuss it at the reunion.

Relieved that he had a plan in place, Chance took a deep breath. Things were already looking up. He turned to his attention to 12-A, and after a moment of quiet prayer, he walked up to the door, opened it, and went inside.

Chapter 3

Garrison Station served as a railroad hub for central Vermont. Located conveniently at the intersection of the town's Vine and Main Streets, Garrison Station maintained its position as the town's central transportation hub. The Green Liner passed through here and ran from St. Olaf's, at the northern part of the state, all the way down to Washington, D.C., via New York and other major East Coast cities. It had been running passenger trains since the mid-19th Century, and aside from some minor upkeep and platform renovation work, had essentially remained the same since it was constructed. The depot featured a red-painted wood-frame building with a gabled roof, as well as a small waiting room where people read the local newspaper while they waited board or pick up passengers who were arriving. A large clock hung above the platform.

At two minutes to twelve, the Green Liner approached Garrison Station. It chugged its way along the track, rocking back and forth as its snake-like body slowed to a halt. Few passengers disembarked from the train – three college-aged girls, an elderly couple, a businessman in a suit, and finally, Michaels.

Dressed in jeans and a gray hoodie, Michaels looked every bit the thief his character projected. He looked around. His face showed four days' worth of stubble, a character dress requirement. He scratched his cheek in thought. This was not exactly first class, and certainly not the type of place Farnsworth would visit unless his plane had to do an emergency landing and undergo repairs.

He watched the passengers connect with those waiting for them. Hugs and kisses were exchanged, and one by one they left for the parking the lot. As they cleared, a lone person remained, his back turned to Michaels.

Michaels knew who it was. He hadn't seen his old friend since graduation, but the erect posture and wiry frame still told him it was Strickler. He was positive of that. Although the clothes didn't seem to fit the person he remembered, the arrogant stance and air of annoyance was the same.

"Strickler? Is that you?"

Strickler turned. His eyes roamed over Michaels, and he let out a long sigh.

"Bernie," he said. "You've put on some weight."

Strickler extended his hand for a formal re-acquaintance gesture as Michaels opened his arms for a hug. The two men looked at each other for a beat before just shaking hands.

"That's the good life for you," Michaels said. "Fat and happy. You know how it is."

Strickler said nothing.

"It's been a while," Michaels continued. "When's the last time since we've seen each other?"

"Graduation," Strickler answered curtly.

"That long. How about that. What is this, satin?"

Michaels fingered Strickler's jacket. Strickler removed Michaels' hand.

"Sharkskin," he said.

"Doesn't seem your taste."

Strickler gave Michaels a once-over. "I can't reciprocate the observation."

"So, where is everyone?"

"If you count the old lady inside, I think you're looking at it. Welcome to East Bumfuck."

"No kidding. It's pretty sticks out here." Michaels looked over Strickler's attire – flashy yellow shirt, dark chino pants, the jacket. He leaned in close. "So, come on. Who are you supposed to be?"

Strickler shook his head. He forgot how boring Michaels was.

"You got the same invitation as me. Guessing is supposed to be part of the fun."

"You can't be serious," Michaels said. "I'll tell you if you tell me."

Before Strickler could respond, a commanding voice interrupted the two men's conversation.

"Knock it off, you two," Farnsworth said. "No conspiring."

The men turned. Farnsworth walked toward them, cane in hand. Next to him was Chance peculiarly dressed in a red satin robe, a dirty white button-down shirt, and un-pressed slacks. Elated, he broke into a huge smile and went over to his friends.

"Bernie! Ted!"

He hugged Michaels tightly, and got a hold of Strickler before the taller man could protest. Farnsworth watched them, his smile dissipating and replaced with the reserved look of a scientist watching the commencement of an experiment.

"What the hell are you wearing?" Michaels asked Chance.

"Ah-ah-ah...On your time, people," he said. "The car's over there. We have a schedule to keep."

The men picked up their bags and headed for the car. Farnsworth used the hook of his cane to snag Chance's arm. Chance raised his eyebrows.

"What happened to you?"

"Skiing accident," Farnsworth dismissed the question quickly.

"You need a hand or something, Neal?"

Farnsworth's eyes narrowed as he looked at his friend.

"Don't men slobbering over each other just turn your stomach, Ethan? Oh wait. I forgot."

Farnsworth flashed Chance an exaggerated wink, then laughed leaving his nervous friend flinching from the remark.

*****

The limousine was to everyone's liking. Farnsworth poured twenty-five-year-old single malt into crystal glasses and passed them out amongst the men. Michaels looked at the amber liquid and set it aside.

"Okay, Neal, what's with all the pageantry already?" Strickler asked. "I'm not an expert at these things, but aren't costumes a little passé?"

"For a man whose wardrobe spans the various shades of grey, I didn't think fashion was your strong suit," Farnsworth replied. "Loose lips sink ships, Doctor. Everything will be revealed over lunch."

"Always the gamesman," Chance said. "Come on, toss us old dogs a bone."

"You want a bone, Ethan? Here –"

Farnsworth slapped Michaels on the forehead.

"Hey!"

"Oh, lighten up. It's not like there are many brain cells left in there to kill, are there?"

"Funny."

Farnsworth gestured to the glass of scotch next to Michaels.

"You haven't touched your drink. Fifteen-hundred-dollar-a-glass scotch too low brow for you, Bernie?" Farnsworth asked.

"I don't drink anymore. I've been sober for eighteen months," Michaels lied. He needed it to sound more impressive than it was.

"Oh, eighteen months," Farnsworth replied. "That is impressive, Bernie. How do you like that? Six-pack Michaels is on the straight and narrow. Now *that* is funny."

Farnsworth laughed. No one else did. Michaels shifted uncomfortably in his seat.

"It's a commitment."

"Well, it's only a commitment if you're committed to it."

"What are you saying, Neal?"

"You telling me that you don't sneak a little drink when no one's judging eyes are around? You know what I'm saying. A pint tucked away for a rainy day. In your briefcase, a drawer some place, maybe your car? Tell me you don't have a little bottle of mouthwash that you always carry on you just in case you have to mask the smell of booze and guilt in your mouth before you head home to the Mrs. and the kiddies."

The remark caught Michaels off-guard. He sat there, incapable of addressing the incredibly accurate but grossly inappropriate comments. Chance and Strickler did not come to their old friend's assistance. They knew better than to speak up lest they receive the same level of attention.

"Just kidding, Bernie," Farnsworth said brightly. "Don't be so sensitive."

"So, this mystery game," Chance said after awkwardness in the air became too much to bear.

"That's very perceptive of you, Ethan," Farnsworth said. "You come up with that on your own or did you actually read the invitation?"

Chance squirmed under Farnsworth's assault, kicking himself for not thinking before he spoke. Michaels tried to rescue his friend.

"Where does it take place?" he asked.

Farnsworth looked at Strickler.

"You didn't tell him? Shame on you, Doctor." He turned his attention out the window looking for something, then he turned to the other two men. "Look out the window. Wait for it... wait for it.... There!"

The three men followed the direction where Farnsworth's finger pointed. Outside, a newly erected sign welcomed visitors to town – EAST BUMFUCK – POP. 1820.

The three friends exchanged looks. East Bumfuck?

Outside the window, the men saw more signs with the new name of the town on it.

"Christ," Strickler said finally. "How much did that set you back?"

"A lot less than a malpractice suit, I'll tell you that."

Strickler flinched. Farnsworth smirked a bit, enjoying watching the man as he writhed in his leather seat.

"You know me, Ted," Farnsworth said after he felt his friend had squirmed for enough time. "If it's something I want, no expense is too great."

East Bumfuck was like any other quaint New England town far removed from any major city of size or note. Vine Street and Main Street formed the primary axis along which most of the commercial and residential buildings were built. The town had one of everything – one dry cleaner, one supermarket, one department store, one Sheriff's station, one barbershop, one library. What made this standout from any other quaint town is the fact that the name "Bumfuck" was on every sign – East Bumfuck Congregational Church, East Bumfuck Volunteer Fire Department, East Bumfuck High School. One thing became immediately clear to the men as they watched the signs roll by – Farnsworth had spared no expense for whatever the "game" was that they were going to play.

The limousine's destination was a farmhouse turned into a bed and breakfast at the outskirts of town. A sign at the beginning of the gravel driveway said THE RED LION INN, although there was no red and no lion to be seen. The farm wasn't large but one that appeared to have served the community with whatever produce it grew in its fields. There was a stable, a small barn and a pen. However, judging from the untended fields and the silence atypical of a working agricultural enterprise, the farm had recently stopped functioning in this capacity. They'd soon find that the stable was vacant, and the small barn was used for storage for the dispatched farm equipment. It had reluctantly embraced its new purpose as a hospitality outlet rather than an agrarian one.

The men got out of the car and took in the lush scenery surrounding them – rolling hills bordered by thick line of trees. Mountains loomed large in the distance. Chance took in the expanse of the environment and whistled.

"Wow," he said. "This is beautiful. Absolutely beautiful."

"Mr. Sensitive," said Farnsworth.

The front door of the three-story house opened, and an old man exited. A crusty New Englander, he was dressed in flannels, corduroys, and a faded red hunting cap. He was in his late seventies but strong from a lifetime of farm work and long hours. He eyed the three strangers before addressing his boss.

"Afternoon, Mr. Farnsworth."

"Right on time, Zeke, right on time. The contestants have arrived."

Chance, Strickler, and Michaels shared a look – contestants?

Zeke approached the men. He looked them over, taking in their odd appearances, as if taking in information and coming up with an immediate decision about them. He let out a gruff, then extended a burly hand out. Strickler shook it.

"Hello, I'm –"

"Dr. Strickler. And that there is Michaels. And the youngish fellow must be Mr. Chance. Welcome to the Red Lion, fellows."

Taken aback, the men did not know what to make of this. Obviously, Farnsworth had prepped the old man well.

Farnsworth relished the men's reactions, the surprise in their eyes, the way their lips quivered in confusion. He prided himself on being able to levy the unexpected on the unwilling and swelled when his objectives were reached.

"Pick up your jaws, people," Farnsworth said. "A closed mouth gathers no flies. Okay, enough slacking. It's picture time. Zeke, if you'd be so kind."

Farnsworth limped to the forefront, surrounding himself with the others. Strickler watched him.

"So, you never told us, Neal. What's the problem there?" He gestured to the cane.

"Too much gabbing," Farnsworth replied, brusquely evading the question. "Okay, boys, let's see those pearly whites. Just like back in the college days."

Zeke held the smartphone awkwardly, obviously unaccustomed with the newest technology.

"Who's a winner?" he asked.

The men's faces showed more confusion just as Zeke snapped the picture. He looked at the shot and smiled.

"Perfect," he said.

*****

The main house was simple and old, the floorboards creaking like an old man's bones. The foyer that lay behind the front door was decorated with knick-knacks and tchotchkes, the kinds you would pick up at a fair or swap meet. The walls were adorned with family photos – some black and white, the more recent ones in color. All the frames were sorely in need of a good dusting.

"The Red Lion was the house Benedict Arnold used as a headquarters during the Revolution," Zeke said.

"Benedict Arnold? The traitor?" Chance asked.

"Not at that time, he wasn't," Zeke snorted. "Back then – 1775 or so – he and Ethan Allen led the attack on Fort Ticonderoga. He was a Colonel back then."

"Oh," Chance said.

"I'll show you to your rooms," Zeke said.

He started the trudge upstairs with the men behind him in tow. Farnsworth watched them follow Zeke like ducks to their mother. The scene made him laugh.

Like the main level, the second floor's walls were filled with photographs and framed needlepoint signs with sayings like "God Bless This Home" and "Amazing Grace". Michaels caught Strickler's eyes. Nodding to the signs, he made a face. Strickler rolled his eyes and looked at Zeke.

There were four doors. Two were side by side. One was on the opposite side of hall. The last was at the far end.

"That over there is Mr. Chance's room. Michaels and the Doctor are side by side. The door at the end is the bathroom and has extra linens if you need something not in the rooms."

"Three men sharing a bathroom?" Strickler asked.

Zeke made a gruff noise.

"No, that's Mr. Chance's bathroom. Yours and Mr. Michaels' rooms have a bathroom between you."

Michaels smiled at Strickler who was less than pleased. He slapped the doctor on the back for good measure.

Chance examined a photo with a younger Zeke and a woman by his side. He had to have been in his thirties then. The woman was what he imagined the wife of a lifetime farmer to look like.

"Where is Mrs. – ah – Zeke?"

Zeke turned to Chance. The old man's face was stone, betraying no emotion.

"Passed on. Some years back," Zeke said. Then a little softer, he added, "Right after my daughter."

Chance's face flushed with embarrassment. He didn't know what to say.

"I'm sorry."

"Nice, Ethan," Farnsworth leaned over and whispered into Chance's ear. "Shall we discuss the morning of September 11 next?"

Michaels slugged Chance on the shoulder. Chance shrugged and mouthed, *how would I know?*

Zeke grunted.

"Anyway," he continued. "After Benedict turned coats so to speak, people wanted to burn this house to the ground to get rid of his memory. But my great-great-great grandfather wouldn't have any of it. He bought the house and made it his home. It's been in the family ever since."

Farnsworth made his way to the front of the men. He guided Zeke toward the staircase.

"Thank you for that trip down amnesia lane, Zeke," Farnsworth said. "We'll be down to get something to eat shortly."

The old man nodded and shuffled down then steps.

"Where's your room," Michaels asked Farnsworth.

Farnsworth smiled smugly. He patronizingly tapped Michaels on the back and directed his attention to another flight of steps at the end of the hall.

"Upstairs, of course. The master suite for the master. Food in an hour, sports? Give you a chance to freshen up. Ta-ta."

Farnsworth limped toward the steps and walked upstairs. The three men watched him go.

"Don't look now, fellas," Michael said. "But I think we have just been dismissed.

Chapter 4

Strickler's room was small, furnished with a bureau, night table, and a desk and chair. Two doors led to a closet and the joint bathroom. He unpacked his bags methodically, re-folding clothes and inserting them into the drawers. He hadn't been there three hours and already the "gang" was back to its old form – Farnsworth taking the lead and the rest of them following him around like puppies eagerly awaiting their next treat.

Strickler shook that thought from his head as he placed his travel medical bag on the floor next to the bureau. He had to remain positive and keep his eyes on the prize. He'd get Farnsworth in a beneficial position and take advantage of it. Strickler smiled – it was a move that even Farnsworth could appreciate.

The years hadn't treated his friends too well, an unsurprising turn of events. Well, Chance looked more or less the same. Sure, he was grayer and there were some crows' feet at the corners of his eyes, but he looked trim and relatively fit for his age. Michaels, on the other hand, was a mess. He turned out much like Strickler had anticipated – out-of-shape, and if he guessed correctly – out-of-work.

Strickler detested his friendship with Michaels. It had started off as a simple business relationship – Michaels was the hook-up for pot and pills and Strickler went to him for some Benzedrine to get through mid-terms during their sophomore year. Farnsworth had brought him into the fold later that year by helping Michaels collect a debt. That act ended up solidifying a tenuous friendship between the four of them. Chance was the first brought under Farnsworth's wing their freshman year. Strickler was approached during Cape Week, the time everyone went to Cape Cod for a week after the last day of classes for beach parties, cook outs, and to consume copious amounts of beer. They all seemed to know Farnsworth independently, or at least of him, and in that coincidence, they ultimately were cemented to one another like bricks, with Farnsworth acting as the mortar. By senior year, they got a two-bedroom off-campus apartment together with Chance and Farnsworth bunking in one room, Strickler and Michaels in the other.

They formed quite the Motley crew – Chance was the effeminate artsy suck-up; Michaels was the low-ambition burnout; Strickler the elitist overachiever; and Farnsworth was, well, Farnsworth. He was the existential enigma, avoiding any and all types of classification and stereotype. Despite his above-average background, he moved seamlessly through the rungs of social classes, a chameleon able to blend when necessary and disengage when appropriate.

Strickler opened the bottom drawer and suddenly froze in place. Rolling at the bottom were two small vials of clear liquid. Confused, Strickler looked around as if he expected someone to pop out of the closet and shout, "Surprise!"

No such entrance occurred. He reached down and removed one of the vials. His hand shook a bit. Is this what he thought it was? He steadied his fingers and unscrewed the top. He sniffed. There was an acidic, vinegar-like smell. Not its purest form to be sure, but still a narcotic that he knew very well. His Fentanyl addiction was a big reason why he found himself in his predicament and why he was here. Therefore, it shouldn't have come as a shock that he was staring at two vials of the drug right now.

The vials at the bottom of the drawer couldn't be a coincidence but no one knew about his addiction. His lawyer had ensured that anyone with any inkling of his little weakness was bought off and slapped with a legally binding non-disclosure.

But still.

Almost in a Pavlovian response, moisture beaded immediately on his upper lip. He quickly wiped it away with the back of one hand as he held the vial in the other. He hadn't shot up in a few weeks, using pills to offset his body's need for the opiate. But now here it was in his hand in all its glory and seduction.

Hello, gorgeous.

Behind him, the bathroom door opened revealing Michaels standing in a film of dirty white tile and a clear shower curtain with faded blue fish.

"I hope you don't have irritable bowel syndrome," he said. "The can is right near my bed."

Strickler subtly palmed the vial to obstruct Michaels' view.

"Great," Strickler said. "Aren't I the lucky one?"

"Don't look at me, pal. You're the one that had to shave his back in college, not me."

Strickler mouths a "ha-ha." Michaels entered the doctor's room without invitation and checked it out.

"By all means," Strickler said.

"Nice digs," Michaels said, plopping down hard on the bed eliciting a look of disproval from Strickler. "Just like mine. Decked out in early bumpkin."

"Is there a reason for this intrusion, Bernard?"

"Nothing. I mean, here we are after all these years. I don't know. It just seems weird. Who would have thought?"

"What do you mean?" Strickler asked.

"I don't think any of us has spoken to each other in years."

"What makes you say that?" Strickler asked.

"I think that would have come out once we all saw one another. It just struck me is all."

"We've all been busy," Strickler said. "At least most of us have."

Michaels let the insult roll off his back.

"Anyway, did Farnsworth strike you today as a bit – I don't know – odd?"

Strickler shrugged. He moved so his back was to the bureau. He deftly opened the draw and slipped the vial back inside.

"Farnsworth has always been Farnsworth," he said. "He barks and we jump. All these years after college, looks like we're still doing it."

"You got that right. 'Ours is not the reason why…'"

"Ours is but to do and die."

The rest of the poem's couplet came from Chance who had opened the bedroom door ajar and poked his head through. He entered the room closing the door behind him.

"I didn't realize this was the common area," Strickler groaned.

"You can't have a pow-wow without all three Indians present," he said.

Michaels made space for him on the bed. Chance sat down.

"Saddle up, Kemosabe," Michaels said. "We were just discussing why the hell we're here."

Chance grabbed a pillow and leaned against it.

"You mean besides just missing us?"

Chance laughed, and the two men shared a smile.

"I almost believed that delivery," Michaels said. "You should act."

Chance shifted uncomfortably.

"I'm strictly a behind-the-camera writer. No spotlight for me."

Strickler cleared his throat to get their attention.

"Maybe the right question to ask is, *why* did we all agree to come?"

An odd question that reflected on Chance's and Michaels' faces.

"What do you mean?" Michael's asked.

Upstairs, Farnsworth's room had been greatly improved in accommodations and amenities. Where the rest of the men's rooms were simple, his was truly a master suite that was more reminiscent of the executive level of a five-star hotel. Near his bed, a side table had an array of prescription bottles. Farnsworth sat on the edge of his bed, his face a grimace of pain. He took a couple of pills and washed them down with bottled water.

Over a speaker attached to a piece of electronic equipment near him, he listened to the voices of the men on the floor below.

"We're here to humor him," Farnsworth heard Strickler say. "When he's tired of us, he'll send us straight home."

"No kidding," Michaels' voice said.

"Maybe he's going to tell us he put us in his will." That came from Chance.

Despite the pain, Farnsworth's face managed a grin. Ethan didn't know how close he was. Maybe the failed screenwriter would surprise him in the long run after all.

"I don't know about that. A joke maybe?" Strickler's voice offered. "You can never tell with his brand of humor."

In Strickler's room, the doctor paced back and forth full of nervous energy. Having his space encroached upon didn't help his feelings of anxiety.

Michaels sat up on the bed.

"Who are we kidding," Michael said. "Farnsworth wouldn't give his own mother a pork chop if she were starving."

"No," said Chance. "She'd have to suffer through one of his games first."

Michaels and Chance laughed.

"So," Michaels said, referencing the clothes that they were wearing. "What kind of game is this really?"

"Isn't it obvious?" Chance said, still catching his breath, trying not to laugh. "If this was a board game, it'd be 'Sorry!'"

*****

After a mid-day meal of cold lamb sandwiches, cheese, and other locally harvested ingredients, everyone retreated to their own private spaces. Chance helped bus the table, bringing in the plates from the dining room table into the kitchen where Zeke filled the sink with soap suds. He took advantage of the situation to learn more about his host.

"That was amazing," Chance said. "It's been a while since I had really fresh food."

"City will do that to you," Zeke said. "You get used to others doing for you what you should be doing for yourself."

He nodded a *thank you* and inserted the dishes into the water. Chance lingered.

"Can I ask you a question?"

"I'm not stopping you."

"How long have you known, Neal?"

"Mr. Farnsworth? Not long at all. He had some big-name Boston lawyer contact me a month or so ago. Wanted to rent the place for a special event. Then he offered a ton of money to make some changes here. And then he made a deal with the town. I don't know what's going on, but I'm guessing that would be why you all are here."

Chance looked around. Out the kitchen window, he saw Bernie walking in the back yard, smoking a cigarette. He looked like he was talking to himself or rehearsing a speech. He was all hand movements.

"About that. Did Mr. Farnsworth give you any idea about what we'll be doing or what we have to do?"

"I'm not sure I'm following you."

"This. The game. I mean, come on – changing the name of the town? That's a bit crazy, right? Even for Farnsworth and I've known him since we were eighteen."

The big man shrugged his massive shoulders. If he cared, he certainly didn't show any inkling of it.

"He didn't make me privy to that if that's what you're hunting for. I don't poke a nose where it don't belong. He made me an offer, I accepted it. Simple as that. What you're all here for, well sir, that doesn't concern me other than providing you three hots and a cot."

"Sure, I understand."

Chance remained in the kitchen, watching Michaels. Bernie the Burnout. That's what Farnsworth called him in college. Well, that's what they all called him. Once Farnsworth labeled a person, it was in everyone's best interest to follow suit or else get tagged with an equally unflattering designation. It never made sense why Farnsworth let Michaels hang around the rest of them. Strickler had a prominent upbringing and was the swim captain and debate team lead. Chance was the editor of the literary magazine and had garnered serious praise from the local papers for the stage plays that he directed.

But Michaels?

Michaels was dumb and lazy, a bad combination. He was a low-level campus drug dealer. He didn't even have the ambition to make any real money. There was another kid in school – Jimmy

Visconti – who paid off most of his college tuition by scalping concert tickets. He'd get a bunch of people to go downtown and buy the most tickets they could for which they were paid beer money for standing eight hours in line, sometimes in the worst of inclement Worcester weather.

And there he was, pacing back and forth like a shark. People paced because of guilt or because there was something on their minds.

What was on Michaels' mind?

*****

Michaels rehearsed his approach to Farnsworth. He contemplated just asking him for the money, despite his failure the first time, but quickly dismissed that idea. Seeing everyone together for the first time in nearly forty years reminded Michaels how vicious Farnsworth could be. Even in college he wondered why he had stayed friends with such an asshole, but knew his friendship was based on fear and not necessarily affinity for Farnsworth and certainly not on mutual respect. To not be friends with Farnsworth risked being an enemy, and if Farnsworth had no problem tearing down his friends, his enemies suffered a worse fate.

It had to seem natural. He had to make it look like it was an opportunity for Farnsworth, not a hand-out. And he had to make sure he delivered it with a devil-may-care attitude. You want to help? Great. You don't, then there would be another bus coming along the opportunity highway. Farnsworth had a ton of money, but he wasn't the only one with full pockets. Michaels had to make sure he understood that.

After repeating his pitch over and over several times, Michaels transformed his insecure shell into a fine veneer of confidence.

"Ah!" Michaels cried out, dropping the butt of his cigarette. It had burned down to the filter, stinging his thumb and forefinger.

Turning around, Michaels stopped in his tracks like a rabbit at the first sight of car headlights baring down on the road. Chance stood at the kitchen window staring directly at him. It was a blank stare, as if Chance was looking through him rather than at him. After an awkward moment, Chance raised a hand in a sign of recognition and left the window.

Among their group, Michaels was closest to Chance, which is to say, they weren't very close at all. Chance and Strickler were brought under Farnsworth's fold and kept there early on, while Michaels was the last addition. While they may have known of one another before Farnsworth (St. Sebastian's was not a big school), their circles never really intersected until Farnsworth made them intersect. From that point on, they came together in an unharmonious union that never extended outside the school year. Summers and holiday breaks, the men scurried back to their home states and cities, never to pick up the phone to touch base or even wish one another a "happy birthday". But once on campus, the three of them obediently found each other even though they were never outwardly "friendly" with one another.

After graduation, when work colleagues would swap funny stories about their college days, Michaels found he had few anecdotes to share. Sure, he was a boozer and a recreational drug user, but there was no humorous inciting incident that occurred prior to or after these moments. Michaels was often alone and tucked into the corner of the bedroom he shared with Strickler imbibing or smoking until everything was a comfortably numb haze.

*****

At three o'clock, tea was served in the "game room" – a former den that had been converted into a recreational area. The room featured two wooden tables with a chess board and backgammon board etched respectively on them, a foosball table, and a pool table. Board games were strewn about the room as well as various decks of American as well as foreign cards – Italian, Muushig, Tarot, Jass, and Preferans – positioned throughout. And of course, Farnsworth Enterprises' finest games.

The group photo that was taken that day was tacked in a place of prominence above the fireplace mantel. The men lingered, waiting around for their friend and host. No one spoke, preferring to focus their attention on the ambience of the room as they drank their bland tea.

"A mystery, boys," Farnsworth said, limping into the room, using his cane to push the door all the way open. "Solve a murder and win a prize."

The men turned their attention to Farnsworth who stood in front of them like the Lord of the Manor.

"I have a question, Neal," Strickler said. "How is this different from any other murder mystery weekend?"

"Pick-pick-pick-pick... No wonder your wife gave you the ol' heave-ho, Doctor," Farnsworth scoffed as he entered the room. "Now, as you know by now, you are all specific characters to the story. That is critical to the game and you are never to break from character during the gaming hours. No one – and I repeat – no one will divulge the identity of your character until the end of the game. Is that understood?"

The three men agreed.

"A bit louder."

"Yes!"

"Good. Rules are important. They are the very fabric of our society. Wouldn't you agree?"

"Question. What if we know who the characters are ahead of time?" Michaels asked.

Farnsworth raised his eyebrows.

"Well, well, well...look who's come to play," Farnsworth said. "If you know ahead of time, just keep it to yourself Einstein. Hush-hush and all that."

"That's it? We play a game, have to solve the mystery, and guess who we are?" Chance said. It seemed rather simplistic to him and was expecting more for someone whose livelihood was in the gaming industry.

"Where's the writer's imagination, Ethan? That's only part of it. Solving the mystery is key. Each day you all will be given a specific clue by me. Your job is to deduce what that clue means and how it applies to the location you're at."

"The plot thickens," said Michaels.

"Once you find the specific object in question, write your initials on the space provided. Scoring will be done in the morning by me."

"Of course," Strickler said. "Who else would it be?"

"I have another question," Chance said. "What if one of us doesn't find the object? How can we go on playing?"

"Well, for one thing, Ethan, sucking up won't help." Farnsworth turned to the room. "If for some reason Alzheimer's sets in, don't fret. All the clues will be displayed here the next day."

Strickler looked miffed. "Isn't that a bit unfair for those that do find the clues?"

"Ah, just because you find the clues, dear Doctor, doesn't mean you know how to put them together correctly. But for you worry warts looking to get a shiny star at the top of your paper, I'll let you in on a little secret. The points are meaningless. They're just for my personal amusement."

Michaels smiled and shook his head disbelievingly. Farnsworth turned his gaze at him, arching an eyebrow.

"Speak, Bernie," he said.

"So, this is the new rage? Games for the rich and famous?"

"Are there any other kind?" Strickler asked sarcastically.

"Take a Valium, Doctor, or something stronger if you got it. People, aren't you getting it yet? The objects – these clues – tell a story. Your job is to figure out what that story is. Someone has been killed. One of you did it. Question is, who?"

Maybe it was the way he said it. Maybe it was the way he looked at each of them, as if his eyes pierced through them and out the other sides. Either way, the men sat quietly, processing the instructions, wondering what the hell was this all about.

When too much silence had passed unchecked, Farnsworth sighed loudly. Chance, who had the better imagination of the men, spoke up. There was one question left unanswered. One that was important to ask.

"So, what do we win if we do?"

Farnsworth smiled wildly. It wasn't a friendly smile as much as one steeped in irony and condescension.

"I was wondering which one of you was going to bring that up. So, what does the winner get for hiking to East Bumfuck to humor me and test this new game pilot? How does one million dollars grab you?"

If there was a pin, and it dropped, the sound would have tolled as loudly as the heaviest cathedral bell. Even Strickler who prided himself on not showing much emotion was openly aghast when he heard the amount.

"Oh? Do I have your attention now?" Farnsworth mused.

"Neal, are you joking?"

"No joke, Doctor. One million dollars. Cash. Wired to whatever account you designate. Sound fair enough for your time?"

Chance spoke up next. The number was too high, too out of the realm of possibility. It seemed just another taunt in an endless array of Farnsworth's jokes. And this one hurt the most because it was exactly what he needed. What they all needed.

"Neal, we're your friends. You couldn't expect us to take that money for playing a game?"

Farnsworth waved him off.

"At some point during each of your pathetic lives, you've come to me with your hands outstretched, looking for some money, a loan, whatever, to get you over a hump, an event, a problem. But a man doesn't get wealthy by giving his gold away. Nor does he preserve his dignity by accepting the handouts from those willing to do so. What I'm offering is more sporting. You want it, earn it."

"That's very generous," Chance said.

"Oh, Ethan. Generosity is for philanthropists. I manufacture games. And this is one of them. Perhaps the best one. Start time is eight o'clock sharp."

Farnsworth headed out the room.

"What's the name of the game?" Michaels asked. It was the first time he spoke upon hearing the news of what the purse contained. Farnsworth turned to him, his face impassive and expressionless.

"Attrition," Farnsworth said, and exited the room.

*****

Farnsworth teed up a golf ball in the back lawn. It was late afternoon, but the sun still shone brightly, unimpeded by clouds. Although spring had officially come a week prior, the weather was just beginning to show the promise of warmth.

He eyed the ball carefully. He was a methodical golfer, more focused on technical precision and execution than for any real love for the game. The golf course was more of a place of business, of networking, and was an excuse to remove businessmen from the purpose of their jobs. To him, golf was one big bore, a game that moved too slowly, with slow people, that offered too few complicating variables to make the sport a worthwhile endeavor.

But the golf range was different. The repetition of each swing provided a person the opportunity to think. Just the person and his thoughts, and in that revelation, Farnsworth could almost – *almost* – give golf a pass. But not entirely.

Behind him, Chance exited the house. He watched Farnsworth hit golf balls. Each swing made Farnsworth twinge a bit. But no sooner had he hit a shot before he immediately teed up another ball. Whatever ailed his leg, he wasn't going to let it stop him from doing what he wanted to do.

Chance looked around. He had left Michaels in the game room and Strickler had retreated to his bed upstairs. For all intent and purposes, Farnsworth was alone and there was no time like the present. He barely took a step forward before Farnsworth addressed him.

"What can I do for you, Ethan?"

The remark caught Chance off-guard.

"How'd you know it was me?"

"Call it a hunch," Farnsworth replied.

"I was wondering if I could speak to you for a moment."

Farnsworth kept focused on the ball. He leveled the head of the club against the ball and then pulled back. In one smooth motion, a dull "clink" sounded, and the white ball was jettisoned into the far part of the field.

"The moment's passing, Ethan," Farnsworth chided.

"I was wondering if you got a chance to read *The Sorrow Man*?"

Another swing. He sliced the chip shot badly. He frowned.

"If you mean that inane ramble of adjectives you sent me weeks ago, then I'm sorry to say, yes. At least, what I could wade through. You know what? Pitiful Man is a more appropriate title, don't you think? More accurate anyway."

Clunk! Another chipped shot went astray.

"Tiger Woods or no Tiger Woods," Farnsworth said. "This is still the dumbest game I ever played."

"You didn't like it?" Chance asked. It was hard to obfuscate the hurt in his voice, a tone that drew Farnsworth to attack the way blood in the water drew sharks.

"Now, there's an astute observation, Ethan. If you would have just incorporated some of that honesty into your writing, you might have something more palatable. Or doesn't writing for pornographic cinema count as intelligent prose now-a-days?"

Chance looked like someone took the air out of him with a sucker punch. He looked away from Farnsworth's penetrating gaze.

"Please. In my letter, I asked you not to mention that."

"Oh, don't worry, Ethan. *They* don't know. Only *I* know. Consider it our dirty little secret."

"Secrets have a way of getting out."

"Aptly said," Farnsworth nodded. He mimed locking his lips with a key and throwing it away. He started to laugh at Chance's reaction.

Deflated, Chance turned back toward to the house. He couldn't believe he put himself into the position to be humiliated again. Farnsworth made him so mad. In college, he had hoped someone would put him in his place, but no one was ever up to that challenge. He would get his though. Chance was sure of it. One thing about scales was that they always balanced out sooner or later. In Farnsworth's case, it looked to be later, but that gave Chance little solace now that he exposed yet another vulnerability to a person that took great pains to fully exploit people's them every chance he got.

"Ethan! Ethan, hold up!"

Chance stopped. He turned around, hopeful. Farnsworth looked at him with a contrite expression on his face.

"Yes, Neal?"

The expression dissipated into a mischievous grin as he turned back into his golf stance.

"Am I turning my hips?"

*****

The living room featured a well-stocked wet bar with a variety of liquors and spirits. Michaels stood looking at the alcohol buffet the way a child looked at pastries in a bakery display case. He could look but he couldn't touch. He shouldn't, anyway.

His eyes followed the colorful labels settling on the true love of his life – bourbon – specifically, Blanton's, his own personal elixir when funds allowed it. He fought the urge to take the bottle and retreat to his room or somewhere private where he could become more acquainted with his old friend.

Strickler stopped himself before entering the living room. He watched Michaels' silent adoration of the spirits before him with a curious amusement. It reminded him of the lab tests he had conducted in college, where he and his partner conducted cognitive-learning tasks on rats to see if they could figure out how to discriminate between "good" and "bad." Even now he watched as Michaels' hand rose to touch a bottle as he struggled with his own internal demons before it fell limply at his side.

Strickler cleared his throat and Michaels immediately thrust his hands in his pockets as he turned around.

"Hey, Ted. Didn't hear you there," he said.

Strickler walked into the room and headed over to the bar to fix a drink. Farnsworth wasn't the only one that knew how to put the screws into someone.

"Drink?" he asked Michaels.

"Don't be an asshole," Michaels replied.

"There are other things here, Bernie," Strickler replied. "OJ? Club soda? When's the last time you had a Shirley Temple?"

"Club soda is fine," Michaels said. "Where's Chance?"

"Last I saw, he was sucking up to Farnsworth. I saw them out the bedroom window. Farnsworth was driving golf balls."

"What were they talking about?"

"Gee, Bern, I don't know. I was in my room. I wasn't out there with them."

"Don't get your panties in a twist," Michaels said. "I was just asking." Michaels dug out a cigarette and lit one. Strickler fanned the smoke.

"You own stock or just trying to keep Phillip Morris in business single-handedly?"

"I swear, you get any funnier my sides are going to burst."

"When we were kids, no one knew any better but now with all the studies and all the lawsuits, you still continue to smoke. It's plain stupid. You might as well put a loaded gun to your head."

Michaels inhaled and held it. He then made a "gun" with his thumb and forefinger and placed it against his temple. When he depressed the trigger, instead of blowing the imaginary smoke from the barrel, he exhaled cigarette smoke instead.

"Same old Bernie the Burnout. You're still a child trying to play in a grown-up's world."

"And you're still the same self-righteous prick whose mouthwash I used to piss into in college, but I don't hold that against you."

Instead of counterattacking, Strickler took his drink and sat down in one of the chairs.

"I ought to have my head examined," he said. "I don't even know why I agreed to come here."

"I do. One million dollars."

"Last time I looked, I had an 'MD' after my name. I'm a surgeon. I don't need the money."

"Apparently you do. You're still here."

Strickler glared. Michaels walked over and patted Strickler on the shoulder.

"Come on, Teddy-boy," he said. "Why the long face? So, you aren't the only one whose life hasn't turned out as expected. Join the fucking club."

Strickler removed Michaels' hand.

"I'm doing fine."

"Not according to Farnsworth."

Irritated, Strickler stood up.

"Why don't you have a drink," he said. "You have a better disposition when you're buzzed."

*****

It was ten minutes to eight. Strickler lay in his bed staring at the Fentanyl vial in his hand. He tilted it back and forth watching the clear liquid slosh in a rhythmic back-and-forth. Dinner had been an awkward affair. The men made minimal talk and were overly courteous to one another. He was sure that Chance and Michaels were thinking about the game, which officially started tonight. What started out as a hoot became suddenly serious, almost dire. If what Farnsworth said was true – and there was no reason to think otherwise – they all needed money at some time or another. And chances are they needed a lot of it. And judging from the starving looks they gave when the prize was announced, they still needed it. The realization of this fact, and the acknowledgement that they all were in a state of desperation, made the game and its spoils very real, and by that fact, the competition became more than just a friendly contest.

Strickler got up and retrieved his medical bag. There inside were the basic tools of the medical profession: low-grade narcotics, an electronic blood pressure machine, a stethoscope, bandages, and a prescription pad. The most important piece was the packet that contained the syringes. He took one out. It was slender, its needle sleek and its' point sharp like the nose of mosquito.

His heart skipped a beat. This must be how Michaels felt when he saw an unlocked liquor cabinet. He hated sharing that common trait with an individual he despised as much as his former roommate. But God, how he wanted a taste. Just a little taste.

Strickler positioned the metal needle at the cap. Just a pop and pull back, it was as simple as that.

Then that pin prick would make everything right in the world.

A booming knock at his door jolted Strickler from his seduction.

"Let's go, Ted! Game time!" Chance's voice summoned him.

Strickler's face deflated. He stood, inspecting his image in the full-length mirror. He looked like a faggot. There was no other way to describe the flashy clothes, the synthetic material. Like he was a boy-toy chicken hawk looking to score a wealthy older man hiding his attraction to eye candy. Was this really worth the money?

The steel glint returned in his eyes.

It damn sure was. For one million dollars, even Strickler would consider sucking a dick. One million dollars would make most people do most things. It was that much money. And once he won it, he'd cut all ties from these people and never look back.

Chapter 5

Darkness had settled in the sky and the night creatures chirped and rustled in the quiet evening air. Outside the inn, the three men stood in a line like mustered soldiers. Each of the contestants held a penlight and slip of paper in their hands.

Farnsworth leaned on his cane near the van that would take the men into town. He watched the men inspect the items he had just passed out to them, relishing in the confusion that registered on their faces.

Strickler spoke first. He read what was written on the paper.

"BA 574.12? What the hell is this supposed to be?"

"Tsk, tsk, Doctor. All that education and you're looking for an easy way to the solution? I expected more from a man that has a 'M.D' after his name."

Strickler shot him a look. Had he overheard his conversation with Michaels?

"Are there any other legitimate questions?" Farnsworth asked the group.

"How much time do we have to complete the task at hand?" Michaels asked.

"Four hours. At midnight, Zeke will pick you up at the designated spot. If you're not there, like

Cinderella, your ride will turn into a pumpkin. Anything else?"

"No," Chance said.

"Decipher the code, and you'll find the object. Find the object, and you're one step closer to finding out who your victim is and the person who committed the crime."

Zeke opened the door of the van. The men start to file toward it.

"Remember – and I can't make this clearer – Zeke'll pick you up at exactly midnight in front of the church. Miss your ride, and it's a mile-and-a-half mile walk back."

They all climbed in. Farnsworth stood by the door.

"You'll be dropped off at different places in East Bumfuck. Then my eager little scholars, you're on your own."

With that, he slammed the door shut.

*****

Zeke dropped off Strickler in front of Barcelo's Store. Signs posted in the window advertised 30 percent sales on all kitchen goods and supplies. It was exactly the type of store Strickler imagined the residents of East Bumfuck – or whatever the town's real name was – would patron.

Strickler looked around. The streets were deserted. The main strip was well lit by streetlamps. No store was open. He was unsure if this was their usual business operations or if Farnsworth "persuaded" them to close early for the sake of the game. He had to hand it to Farnsworth – if a rube setting was the intended ambience, he certainly nailed it on the head.

He hated playing games.

In college, he avoided them like the plague. Beer Pong, Quarters, Zoom-Schwartz, Thumper, The Century Club...he never understood their attraction. They got people drunk quicker, but who needed a game to do that? It never stopped anyone from seeing how fast or how much they could drink. They were for people like Bernie the Burnout. Even Farnsworth eschewed them. They had that in common.

But here he was just the same. If drinking games were banal, games like this – games in general – were complete wastes of time. Play a game? Try reading a book.

And now, at his age, he was playing another game. The difference was the money. Big money.

He needed to beat Chance and Michaels. He thought he could, that he *should*. But his mind didn't work this way. He was too literal, too technically-orientated. He didn't solve puzzles. He didn't like mysteries. He didn't like...people.

Strickler regarded the slip of paper and penlight and shook his head. What the hell was he going to do with this?

"Decipher the code...Decipher the code," he said. "Fucking, Farnsworth."

*****

Michaels found himself on a corner of an intersection a few blocks away from the center of town. He was dumped in an area where the commercial real estate ended, and the residential homes began. He immediately lit a cigarette and took a long drag as he gathered his thoughts.

"Come on, Bern. Think...Think..."

But nothing came to mind.

If he ever needed a drink, it was now. Alcohol got the juices flowing. But even he knew that it wouldn't be one isolated drink; he'd start off that way then work his way down the bottle until he forgot what he was doing outside in a middle of a town called East Bumfuck.

He laughed despite himself. It was too on the mark.

So was the prize. One million dollars. That was a lot of dough. That was substantially more than he was going to ask Farnsworth for in the first place. That would pay everyone's college, grad school, weddings, hell, even homes. That money was redemption. That money would buy him back into his family's good graces and maybe even a little more.

Michaels smiled to himself. Farnsworth was one smart mother. Sure, the total combined money that the men had asked him for had to be much less than the prize on the table now. But by elevating the amount to that level, Farnsworth was assured that they would play the game, no matter how infantile it seemed to them. He'd guaranteed that they would do exactly what he wanted them to do, when he wanted them to do it.

And it raised the stakes.

One million dollars was a game-changing amount. It's what resurrected people's lives. It made people do things. Bad things.

Thing was, Michaels would have to win the game to get it.

He had to.

Though he wouldn't admit it, Michaels was very bright. In high school, he was salutatorian without ever hitting the books hard. Academics came naturally to Michaels, and as often what happens when people don't have to exert effort, he was content to place second when a little mental elbow grease would have let him claim the top spot. Not having to work hard, Michaels robustly explored other interests like smoking weed and drinking beer. College was his coming out. He never studied. In fact, he was high more days than not, and he passed all of his classes without showing up to class with any regularity. In this way, he was a textbook underachiever, a moniker he wore like the meatball-stained pajama top he wore to morning classes as a sloppy badge of honor.

Michaels swore and started to march in the direction of the closed shops, moving away from the darkness and into the streetlamp light.

*****

Chance stared at the store front of a greeting card and stationary shop. "East Bumfuck Stationary" blinked bright red neon, lighting up his face in a candy-apple red. This obviously wasn't the key to solving the puzzle. That would not suit Farnsworth's need to see you squirm like a worm on the end of a hook before giving you your prize, whether that be money for a keg party's cover charge or a one-million-dollar windfall.

He thought he had a leg up on the other two. Strickler was strictly an in-the-box-thinker, and Michaels had burned too many brain cells in college.

But he was a creative thinker. And puzzles – mysteries – were creative in how they were constructed, and therefore benefitted from creativity to deconstruct them.

So, why had this clue stumped him?

BA 574.12. What was that supposed to be? And why would that be in a town like East Bumfuck?

Chance smiled. He had always appreciated Farnsworth's sense of humor, and the re-naming of the town was just another example of how his wit could be biting as well as straight to the point. The town played in this little storyline somehow, he was sure of it. Farnsworth would not – did not – just throw in things if they didn't matter on some level. In that knowledge, Chance felt that he had an edge. That detail, no matter how seemingly trite, was a piece of the puzzle. He didn't know how just yet, but he would. He was a writer. He had an imagination. And that's what set him apart.

Chance surveyed the area. His imagination wasn't helping him just now. And so, he eeny-meeny-miney-moed a direction and pursued it.

*****

Strickler wandered down a side street and saw the lights of a convenience store on. Finally, someone was up and about around this sleepy town. He hustled over to the front door where he saw two men – Indians or Pakistanis he assumed from judging their complexion – behind the counter. He immediately went inside.

The two men were in a heated debate about something in their native language. The staccato rhythm of their speech sounded harsh, almost as if they were swearing at one another. Strickler tried to get their attention.

"Excuse me...? Excuse me...? Hello?"

The men were shouting at each other, their faces flustered and their arms flailing in all kinds of directions.

"Hey!" Strickler slammed his hand on the counter. The men immediately stopped and turned their attention to Strickler. They gave him a disapproving look, and Strickler immediately understood that his attire was different and that he, not them, stuck out like a sore thumb here.

"Do you know what this is?" He held out the paper. The men exchanged a brief discourse. The older one took the slip of paper, looked at it, and shrugged. He passed it to his friend who did the same. They handed the paper back to Strickler.

"You buy something?" the younger one asked. He had a thick accent.

"What? No, I just want to know what this is," he replied.

"No talk. You buy, or you go," the older one said, with an equally thick accent.

"I'm just looking for some help," he said. "You know, help. *Help.*"

He tried pantomiming what "help" was but looked ridiculous. The two men took a step back from Strickler. One got closer to the phone.

"You buy something or leave," the younger man ordered.

Strickler took a step forward. The older man picked up a telephone and started to dial someone. Strickler thought it might be the cops.

"Okay, fine. I'm leaving. I'm leaving," Strickler said loudly to make the old man put down the phone.

Strickler turned and headed out the door. The two men waited, watching him walk past the store.

The younger man came around the counter and went out the front door to see if he had gone.

Satisfied, he walked back into the store.

"Douchebag," the young man said, in perfect unaccented English.

The two men laughed aloud.

*****

Chance remembered a book he read when he was a kid. He couldn't remember the title, but the story was a mystery in which a character being hunted by a killer hid evidence in a bus station locker and mailed the key with the locker number to his sister. The key and the number were a puzzle she had to solve as the killer turned his attention to her.

Keys and bus stations. A classic mystery formula.

Chance spotted a pay phone. He went over to it hoping he'd find a phonebook attached by metal chord. He was in luck. Small town American crime and vandalism hadn't made its way into this rural Nirvana. The phonebook was there, and what's more, it was pristine. There wasn't an ounce of dirt on the pages, and the booth was absent of any stench of urine or feces.

He opened the phone book, quickly flipping through the pages until he found what was he looking for – East Bumfuck Bus Station.

Bingo.

He wrote down the address, slammed the book shut, and started to look for Grey Hounds and Peter Pans.

*****

Michaels stood outside a pawn shop. Through the bars on the windows, he saw a large pot-bellied man behind the counter with a baseball cap featuring a Mack Truck logo. Michaels puffed on his cigarette thoughtfully, before tossing it aside, and walking inside.

The shop was small by pawnshop standards. Shelves held a variety of items in all shapes and sizes. It seemed to have one of everything, which made it seem to Michaels that it was an interpretation of what a pawn shop should be, rather than what one was. It was also less protected. Where he was from, pawnshops protected whoever worked behind the counter with two inches of thick bulletproof glass. Here, the clerk just leaned against the counter flipping through a hunting magazine.

The man looked up from the counter and narrowed his eyes when Michaels walked through the door. His hand instinctively moved slowly to something under the counter. At first puzzled, Michaels realized that this was a reaction to the way he was dressed. He looked like a thief and this guy wasn't taking any chances. He lifted his hands up to show that he was not carrying any weapons.

"Can I ask you a question?" he asked as he stepped forward.

"You can ask it where you're standing," the large man replied. Juice from his chewing tobacco ran down one side of his mouth.

"I need to show you some numbers and see if they are from your store. I'm going to put my hand down my front pocket slowly, okay?"

The large man said nothing and just nodded. Michaels did what he said, and slowly produced the slip of paper and carefully set it on the counter and took a step back.

Suspicious, the large man snatched the paper with one hand, keeping his other hidden behind the counter.

"What the hell is this supposed to be?" the large man asked. He spat a wad of juice onto the floor beside him.

"I was hoping you could tell me that."

"Well, I can't. This isn't from any of the claim tickets I use here, if that was what you were thinking," the large man said, handing him back the slip of paper

Michaels face deflated.

"Do you know of anywhere else that might use a code like that?"

The large man eyed Michaels. He spat again on the floor.

"You an idiot, or something?"

"Excuse me?"

"I'm asking if you use that head for anything more than keeping those ears apart?"

Michaels didn't get what he was saying. The large man sighed.

"Stop doing the doobie and get your mind straight. It's like you never even heard of the library."

"Library?"

"You know, big building with lots of books? You ain't the brightest crayon in the box, are you buddy?"

"What?"

"Ever hear of the Dewey Decimal system, Einstein? That's third grade shit right there."

"Dewey Decimal..." Michaels said, finally illuminated. "Thanks."

Michaels headed out the door. The large man smirked. His hand came up from behind the counter with a package of Twinkies. He opened it, dug one out, and shoved it into his mouth.

Outside, Strickler watched Michaels leave. He quickly intercepted him.

"Is this it? Is this place?"

"I'm not holding your hand. Go and figure out yourself."

"Thanks a lot."

Strickler entered the pawn shop while Michaels hustled down the street.

*****

Chance stood outside the bus station. There was a grave uneasiness on his face. He hated busses. He hated bus stations more. They were godless places, located on the fringes of a town, pushed to the side and out of immediate eyesight. They catered to the worst humanity had to offer. People that arrived or departed on busses generally left one shitty existence and headed toward another.

He was looking at the bus station but remembering a time in his past of which he wasn't proud. For eighteen months when he was unemployed, he worked at a bus station just like this. Not at the ticket counter or even sweeping the filthy floors, but in the men's bathroom, where men exchanged sexual favors for drugs and money. That's where he met Tom, and after a ten-minute oral act, he was given a job as a writer with his company.

Looking at the hulking concrete structure caused Chance to shudder.

He took out the paper slip and walked inside.

Two homeless men stretched out on benches, their worldly possessions contained in several black plastic trash bags. He walked by them quietly as he headed for his intended destination – the locker area. He checked the number on the paper slip and searched for the corresponding number on the lockers. He found 574 and tried to open it.

"Shit," Chance said. It was locked. He tried the other ones surrounding it, but all were locked.

"Hey, you need some help?"

Chance turned to see a man in his thirties, slender, unshaven, and who probably hadn't had a meal or a shower in a few days.

"No, I'm fine, thank you," Chance said.

"I think I know what you're looking for," the man said. "I can help."

"You can? Where is it?" Chance said. The hope in his voice was unmistakable, but he was desperate for a lead.

The man looked around the desolate station to make sure no one else was in earshot.

"What's it worth to you?"

"What?"

"Exchange of goods and services, trickle-down economics, I don't know, whatever you want to call it. You help me, I help you."

"I don't have any money," Chance said. He wasn't lying. They were told by Farnsworth that they could not have any money or identification on them when the game was in motion.

"You got a mouth, don't you?"

"What do you mean?"

"You know…suckee-suckee. You do that, I'll take you personally to the thing."

Chance contemplated the offer for a split-second. One million dollars would get most of the straightest guys on their knees. But he caught something in the man's eyes. He had been in this position before, except he was in the guy's position instead of the one he was in now. Seeing himself, Chance recognized the con.

"Nice try," Chance said, pushing past the man as he walked by.

*****

Michaels quickly walked down the street. He moved with purpose, constantly looking both left and right with the nervous energy of one racing against the clock.

"Where are the damn street signs?" he said to himself. He came to a four-way intersection and took a right to get back on the main road.

Michaels froze. There on the opposite corner, a sheriff's deputy's car idled. It was either a speed trap or just East Bumfuck's finest killing time until their shift was over. He didn't imagine much crime happened in this town and by extension the cops were more municipal officials that rescued animals or helped direct traffic when the streetlights didn't work.

Michaels hadn't done anything wrong, but based on the reaction from pawnshop guy, he didn't want to waste time with the local authorities when he had only about thirty minutes until the game ended for the night.

Before he moved, the cop car turned its flood light on, bathing Michaels in a bright, white light.

"You, over there! Stay where you are!"

Michaels shielded his eyes. He heard the deputy's car door open, and the sound of boots on the ground.

"What's your business here?" the deputy said to him. He flashed a bright light on Michaels who had to shield his eyes with his hand.

"I'm visiting," Michaels said. "We're playing a game, and we're just out here..." He stopped when he realized how ridiculous he sounded.

"Visiting, eh? From where? It's a bit late for sight-seeing, not that there's much to see here anyway."

"I haven't done anything wrong," Michaels said.

"We'll see about that. Keep your hands where I can see them."

The deputy moved closer. Michaels had to decide – deal with the local-yokel and miss finding the clue, or else bolt.

There was no reason to stay put and one million of them to make fast tracks.

Decision made, Michaels took off down a side street.

"You! Freeze!"

He could hear the deputy behind him, gaining ground. He couldn't remember the last time he jogged, no less running a full sprint for his life. But fight-or-flight was very much alive in him, and despite the sharp pain stabbing his lungs, his legs continued to pump with conviction.

Emerging from the side street, Michaels turned an immediate left, a bad decision as he ran into a chain link fence.

"Shit!" He looked around frantically – he was stuck at a dead end. Up was the only place to go. Up and over some barbed wire.

He wrapped his fingers around the chain link and started to climb. His fingers throbbed from bearing the weight of his body. He grunted, gritting his teeth as he concentrated on putting the toe of his shoe firmly in place before raising the other, getting it secure and pulling himself up a notch. His muscles burned with the effort, but he made progress.

He was halfway up the fence when the deputy came out of the side street.

"Stop!" he shouted at Michaels.

Michaels hesitated a second before summoning up the rest of his strength to get over the barbed wire. The sharp barbs snagged his jeans and hoodie, but the weight of his body and the laws of gravity brought him hard to the ground on the other side. His clothes were torn, and his skin was cut, but he had made it. He gave himself a second to recuperate before scurrying away from the fence.

The deputy made the fence in time to see Michaels disappear into the darkness. Then he produced a joint from his pocket and lit it.

*****

Michaels stayed behind a row of bushes, watching the street. It was quiet. If the cops were following him, they hadn't made it here, at least not yet. Across the street, the East Bumfuck Public Library looked more like a three-story schoolhouse than a library. The front steps were wide and led up to a set of heavy doors. Large elm trees flanked either side of the entrance. If the sign wasn't out front, he could easily have mistaken this for a home.

Michaels hustled toward the library, keeping low and moving along the tree shadows on the ground. He crawled up the front steps to the front door. After a final check around him, he grabbed the handle.

"Here goes nothing," he said.

He pulled once, expecting it to be locked.

It wasn't.

Michaels quickly slipped inside and closed the door behind him moments before the headlights of the slowly creeping sheriff's deputy's car crawled by, shining search lights in the dark thickets by the road.

The library was completely pitch black save for the moonlight streaming in from large windows. There was no alarm system and no emergency lighting. Michaels found his penlight and turned it on, running the beam over the main floor to get his bearings. The clock on the wall said it was twenty minutes to twelve.

Attrition

In the center of the room, an elevated librarian's desk provided a holistic view of the surrounding tables. Michaels walked over to it, searching the drawers for information on how the library was organized. Moving around the papers and files on the desk revealed what he was looking for – a taped guide of the library's layout broken down into the Dewey Decimal classification system.

The 500s were on the third floor – Pure Sciences.

Michaels found the stairwell and raced up the four flights. At the top of the stairs, per a hand-dawn map, the floor was categorized in the following way:

500 Natural Science	560 Paleontology
510 Mathematics	570 Life/Human
520 Astronomy	Sciences
530 Physics	580 Plants
540 Chemistry	590 Animals
550 Earth Sciences	

Michaels hustled to find the Life/Human Sciences section. He moved quickly down the stacks of books, trying to match the number on the slip of paper to a book on the shelf. His eyes roamed over the numbers and titles until he found what he was looking for – a well, worn college Biology textbook.

Removing it from the shelf, he opened it and read the following:

"Looks who's coming up in the world! You've made the Dean's list and moved to the head of the class."

Even Farnsworth's writing was dipped in sarcasm. Michaels should have felt elated for being the first to discover the clue, but a chill ran up Michaels' spine. It wasn't quite the reaction he was expecting.

"Sign your initials," a woman's voice called out to him.

Michaels spun around to see an old woman sitting in the darkness. She was blind and almost witch-like with her long white hair and gravelly voice. She just sat there, rocking quietly. Michael searched for a something to write with, but the woman was one step ahead of him. Her outstretched withered handheld a pen. Michaels took it and signed the book.

"You can leave now," she said, and Michaels, like before, did as he was told.

Exiting the library, Michaels ran into Strickler, who pressed a cold soda can against his eye.

"Where'd you get that?" Michaels said, gesturing to the red mark under his friend's eye.

"A disagreement over the health risks of chewing tobacco," Strickler said.

"I meant the soda. You weren't supposed to have any money on you."

"I didn't," Strickler said.

Michaels' face broke into a grin. The theft of something so small was beneath Strickler and Michaels knew it. And in this knowledge, Michaels felt it more than appropriate to needle his friend.

"Watch out, Ted. That's how it starts. A soda here and there, and before you know it, you're committing armed robbery."

"You're a waste of skin," Strickler said.

"At least I didn't come in second – again," Michaels retorted.

Strickler shot him the evil eye. It was a reference to a secret wager they had made in college. One that Michaels did not forget and that Strickler could never live down.

Strickler let out a disgusted sigh before going up the stairs into the library.

*****

Outside the church, the old crusty Vermonter checked his watch. He was getting antsy. It was bad enough he had to put up with this silly nonsense, but he was not getting paid to be at these men's beck and calls.

"That's it. Orders are orders," Zeke said to Strickler and Michaels as he slid open the van door for the men to get inside.

"Give him another minute, Zeke," Michaels said.

"Mr. Farnsworth expects people to follow his directions."

"Who are you telling? Try living with the son-of-a-bitch."

Zeke grumbled something, then climbed into the front seat. He wasn't taking any gruff from these two men. Their names weren't on the check he cashed. He started the van. Strickler hopped in the back.

"I'm not walking," he said to Michaels. "You coming?"

Michaels was about to follow him inside when a truck came down the road and stopped near the van. They watched as Chance hopped out of the passenger-side door and ran over to the van.

"Thanks, buddy," he said to the driver after he had climbed inside.

"You just made it," Michaels said to him when Chance climbed into the van. "Old MacDonald was ready to leave you high and dry."

"What happened to you?" Strickler asked, looking over Chance's disheveled appearance.

"Don't ask. Who found it?

Strickler and Michaels both raised their hands. Chance groaned.

"You're kidding me. Where was it?

"You know we can't say," Strickler said after an awkward silence.

"Don't worry, buddy. You'll see it tomorrow," Michaels said.

Another sigh from Chance who turned to look out the window as the van left town into the oncoming darkness.

Chapter 6

Michaels was exhausted. A hot shower and a thorough scrubbing of his teeth wasn't enough to wipe away the night's indecency. He wanted to shave but remembered that wasn't a part of his character. And while he understood that it was important to stay in character, he felt that the clothes were enough and everything else was just earrings on an overly made-up pig.

He finished up and headed down the hall to his room. Strickler had "called" their shared bathroom for a long hot bath. He didn't feel like putting up a fight. That old woman in the library had given him the creeps and he just wanted to put as much distance in his mind between him and the entire library.

He paused by Chance's door to see if he could hear his friend stirring inside. Chance had a tough go of it this evening and he wouldn't let him or Strickler know what happened. Whatever it was, it had shaken him a bit, and that may have been enough to make him beeline for his room when they got back to the inn, and why he didn't mind Michaels jumping ahead of him for a shower. Farnsworth was not to be found when they got back. While it was late, he still had expected the lord of the manor to have been waiting for them to hear of who succeeded, and more importantly, who did not. His lack of presence just seemed, well, odd. He was not the type of person that let an opportunity to ridicule his friends go by so easily.

Michaels locked the door of his room. Though he was tired, adrenaline had not completely left his veins. He removed his t-shirt and checked out his physique in the mirror. He squeezed the spare tire around his waist; what used to be two pinches of fat could now be grabbed by the whole hand. Getting old sucked.

He went over to the bureau to change t-shirts into something more comfortable. He opened the top drawer.

He didn't expect to see what he saw, but two things were certain.

It wasn't his.

And where it came from, he didn't know.

Michaels withdrew the metal flask. It was resting right on top of his clothes, as if someone had just laid it there as part of the turn-down service.

Flasks hold booze, and shaking it in his hand, Michaels knew it was full.

His fingers shook a bit as he unscrewed the cap. He lifted it to his nose and took a slight sniff.

Bourbon. Of course, his favorite. Michaels inhaled again, this time more deeply, and then one more time to have the smell of alcohol burn his nostril hair. He capped it and dropped it back into the drawer and slammed it shut.

Who put this here?

*****

After his bath, Strickler checked his cheek in the mirror. That Neanderthal's punch didn't catch him squarely, but what had landed hurt badly. He had never been one for fights, preferring to ignore the irrelevant than engage them, letting his silence and indifference cut down his adversaries for him. That worked in college to some extent and in his professional life, but not in a place where people prided themselves on curt answers. This kind of town did not conform to the dictates of normal social constructs such as class and economic standing.

He almost didn't find the clue. That got under his skin more than the punch. Strickler was a surgeon for Christ's sakes. He had an intellect few possessed, and this was just a stupid game. Albeit, one with considerable rewards for the winner, but still a game, nonetheless. He shouldn't have struggled with the clue this evening. In retrospect, the call number was simple; he should have recognized it immediately as being a library categorization. There wouldn't be any more mistakes, he promised himself. He wouldn't lose to Chance or Bernie the Burnout.

Laying back on the bed, Strickler wondered about the game. What was with the textbook? What kind of puzzle could this be? Truth be told, he didn't care about the game, only what the game promised. That and enduring Farnsworth's assaults for the next

couple of days. He could withstand those barbs –
within reason – as long as he was the one that walked
away with one million bucks in his pocket. Hell, he'd
even hire a thug to put a hurt in Farnsworth's other
leg.

It plagued him to have to salute smartly to
that insipid blowhard.

One day he'd have Farnsworth where he
wanted him, and then they'd see if he'd be such a
smart aleck then. Farnsworth on his knees and
cowering, it brought a smile to his face. He'd love to
break Farnsworth down, penetrate that Maginot Line
that he had erected to separate him from everyone
else, and systematically deconstruct his attitude, his
smug self-confidence, his humanity.

Strickler laughed out loud. It was such an
unfamiliar and spontaneous action that he startled
himself.

*****

Chance lay on his bed naked and curled
tightly into a ball. Was the man at the bus station real
or was he a plant by Farnsworth? It didn't seem that
far-fetched; after all, Farnsworth spent a boatload of
money to get the town to change its name and to get
Zeke to quit farming, so why not hire an actor or two?
It professionalized the whole experience, so to speak.

But no one knew about that part of his life,
certainly not any of the people here. There was no
way Farnsworth could have guessed that. It was a

coincidence, he reassured himself, nothing more. It had to be.

Still. It didn't make him feel better. It made him remember and Chance hated to remember things like that. Sure, he had slept with men. He still did. That was true. But those eighteen months he wasn't a gay man looking for comfort; he was a lab rat who could be thrown into any experiment to do anything if the price was right.

If that wasn't bad enough, he didn't find the clue tonight. Yes, Farnsworth said that finding the clues didn't matter technically – it was for sport, for bragging rights. But he knew that his failure to write his initials would elicit the sarcastic attention of their benefactor. Just because he was Farnsworth, everyone had to sit still and just take it. And he was sick of that. He was sick of being the butt of jokes. He was sick of the gay innuendos and smug superiority that Farnsworth lorded over him like an executioner. He was sick of just taking it.

There was a reason why such close college friends went their separate ways after graduation. Farnsworth may not have been the only reason, but he was one of the main ones. Chance bet that if he asked Michaels or Strickler they'd admit to that as well.

Farnsworth pissed him off so much. If there was a God, He would allow Chance to be there when Farnsworth got his. Chance almost wanted that more than the one-million-dollar payday. To see

Farnsworth's face smeared in shit, literally or figuratively.

The thought of that made Chance smile. He got up from the bed, dressed in his pajamas, and climbed under the sheets.

Farnsworth dead or destroyed. Either one suited him just fine.

*****

The next morning the men convened in the dining room for breakfast. A stand near the window displayed the worn old biology textbook like a sacred text. Chance sat at the head of the table, drinking a cup of coffee. Every now and then he glanced over at the book as if he was trying to listen to what it whispered to him. Michaels focused on devouring the scrambled eggs and bacon on his plate, helping himself to the extra bacon at the table that only he seemed interested in putting in his belly. He had a way of eating that made you take notice. He'd fork in a mound of eggs, followed by a bacon strip, crunching them together in his mouth before washing it all down with a loud slurp of orange juice. He repeated the action several times, eliciting a disgusted look from Strickler.

Farnsworth looked fresh and reinvigorated. He walked back and forth with the aid of his cane, conducting his own after-action review of the men's efforts the previous night.

"A point for Michaels and Strickler," he said. His voice was upbeat and animated with no signs of the fatigue it had shown the previous evening. He rapped the table to get Michaels' attention. "Bernie, well done. Well done, indeed."

Michaels looked at the other men, then turned to finish his plate. Farnsworth put a consoling hand on Chance's shoulder.

"And for you, Ethan, a disappointing zero. The big, fat proverbial goose egg. It's a good thing you don't write detective stories. The good guys would never solve a crime."

"About last night, Neal," Michaels interjected once he swallowed his food. "I was almost arrested. If we aren't allowed to have ID or carry money, there needs to be…"

He stopped when he saw Farnsworth mime playing an imaginary violin.

"What are you doing?" Michaels asked.

"If you cry me a river, Bernie, I think it best to play you a song."

Michaels looked at the other men. Chance rolled his eyes. Strickler dismissed him. He pushed back his plate.

"Okay," he said. "What's in store for today?"

"Tonight," Farnsworth corrected him. "The day is yours. But the night, that's all mine."

"Why do we always have to play at night?" Strickler asked, perturbed.

"Because, Doctor," Farnsworth said. "That's when bad things happen."

"Look, I get what you're saying," Michaels said, "but what I was thinking…"

"What'd I tell you about that, Bernie? Thinking only gets you into trouble. Now, as I was saying before your mouth spit out your foot, was that…"

Farnsworth didn't finish the sentence because he doubled over in pain. It was an intense sharp pain that started from his chest and like a compass, shot off in all directions. He dropped to his knees, somehow barely managing to keep on hand on the table preventing his total collapse. The men looked on frozen, not knowing what to do or what to make out of his sudden show. Was this another spectacle or something else?

After watching him endure the attack a little longer, Strickler went over to him.

"Neal? What's wrong? Where's the pain?"

Chance and Michaels watched Farnsworth during this moment of weakness. The two men caught each other's glance, and Chance could have sworn he saw a hint of a smile tug at the corners of Michaels' mouth

Farnsworth studied Strickler's face. There was a hint of humanity in that moment of helplessness as he fought to catch his breath. He reached out and patted Strickler on his chest to let him know he was alright, before shoving the doctor away. Strickler lost his balance and fell backward onto his ass. Farnsworth then dug out a pill case from his pocket and consumed two small pills. The men watched with a morbid curiosity to see the effect the pills had. Slowly, Farnsworth's breathing became regular. When he felt up to it, he stood up, gradually letting the hand that had helped him steady himself, leave the reassurance of the tabletop.

Chance spoke up first. He said what was on everyone's mind.

"You mind tell us what that was all about?"

Farnsworth's impenetrable veneer quickly returned. With one hand he brushed back his hair and smoothed out his shirt and pants.

"Nothing, Ethan. Just a little ulcer. Everything's fine."

Chance looked at Strickler who subtly shook his head. That was no ulcer.

"Gentlemen, I'm going to lie down for a bit. Feel free to have the run of the inn, and if you're so inclined, head into town."

"Maybe we should call off the game tonight?" Michaels said.

Farnsworth whipped around. There was anger in his eyes, an unusual reaction for someone that seemed so detached of emotion.

"No. Once it's started, it can't be retracted. Understand that? All of you. Promise me that no matter what, the game doesn't stop. No matter what."

The men didn't know what to make of this uncharacteristic show of feeling. It made Farnsworth seem more – accessible – and not the untouchable larger-than-life presence that influenced their actions with the ease of pulling a puppet's string.

"Agreed," Strickler said.

"Of course," said Michaels.

"Yes, Neal," Chance offered.

Farnsworth smiled. The condescension returned once they all immediately and obediently answered the way he wanted them to answer.

"Good," Farnsworth said, and he limped out of the dining room.

*****

Chance sat on the large rocking chair on the front porch with his laptop computer. He had started a new novel, an idea borne of the reunion of college friends in a remote location – a beach house in this initial draft – and an offering made by the richest of the group to give each of them a substantial amount of money. The men were estranged, having little-to-no contact with one another for so many years before meeting up now for – what? That was what he was stuck on. What would bring friends like these – friends like the ones that were inside the house beside him – to come together after so much time had passed.

Chance typed one word in the document.
Money.

He then continued typing.

...is the root of all evil...makes the world go 'round...is no object...talks, bullshit walks...

He looked at what he had written before hitting the backspace and erasing the words from the screen.

Near the detached garage, Zeke tinkered under the hood of an old '55 Ford blue pickup truck. Chance's father had owned a mechanic's shop and had an appreciation for classic cars. Chance had worked with him during his high school years for extra money – rotating tires, replacing batteries, and changing oil. His father threw him in the deep end and let him flail about until he could tread water. He would be damned if he was going to have any son of his rely on roadside service if his wheels gave out. Chance knew his way around an engine block, and he contemplated giving the old man a hand.

Behind him, Michaels walked out and lit a cigarette. He watched Zeke before addressing Chance.

"What do you think about that?"

Confusion crossed Chance's face.

"Zeke fixing the truck?"

"No, I mean before. With Farnsworth."

"That was disturbing. He looked in pretty rough shape," Chance said.

"I don't know. I first thought that," Michaels said. "But the stumbling and chest clutching, I don't know. It seemed a bit staged to me."

With anyone else, Chance would have said that Michaels was crazy, but because it was Farnsworth, it did merit some consideration.

"You think he was faking that?"

"Maybe."

"What for? That would be a little uncouth for a joke, don't you think?"

"Everything is a joke with him," Michaels countered. "He's playing an angle."

Chance mulled this over. The attack, or whatever it was, *seemed* legitimate. It even garnered a reaction from Strickler, and he was a doctor. He shook his head.

"I don't think so. That's a bit extreme, Bernie. There doesn't seem a point."

"You don't? You never know what's staged, what's not, who's on his payroll. I mean, you just have to look where we are at. East Bumfuck – really? Think about it, Ethan. Everyone's a character in his fucked-up world. Everyone can suddenly become important or unimportant dependent on his whim."

Michaels exhaled a trail of blue smoke from his mouth. He nodded over at Zeke who was oblivious to their conversation.

"Look at that poor bastard," Michaels said. "I wonder what role he plays in all of this."

"You think Zeke is involved?"

"Maybe not purposefully, but when was the last time Farnsworth ever left a loose thread unaccounted for? Remember senior year when

Farnsworth offered me a five hundred bucks to spend the night in the tower?"

"Right...the old exorcism chamber. How could I forget? He planned everything to the smallest detail. He hired that special effects company out of Boston. They took care of the smell, the sounds, the shadows... He knew how to play on your fears."

"On all of our fears. It's like he has a thousand wheels in his head churning out ways to screw with you. That's why I don't necessarily buy his act in there. Everything he does is for a purpose. Everything is for his amusement. If I know anything about Farnsworth, I know that."

Chance nodded. As much as he wasn't entirely convinced, Michaels made a good point. Farnsworth was nothing if not an enigma.

"So, why do we put up with it?"

Michaels smiled and stubbed out his cigarette on the railing.

"Because after he has his way with us, after all of the ridicule and humiliation, he picks us up and smooths over all of the rough spots. Then he pats us on our heads and sends us on our way."

"One million dollars smooths over a lot of rough spots," Chance said. "Lord knows I could use it."

"No kidding. Who couldn't?"

*****

Farnsworth reclined in a chaise lounge. Although he was dressed in slacks and a button-down shirt, a silk bathrobe was wrapped loosely around him. His face was taut and grim, a man obviously fighting an insurmountable pain deep within him.

A knock at the door got his attention. Farnsworth regained his composure, grabbing a newspaper. His face turned completely unemotional, maintaining his image of leisurely indifference. He allowed a second knock on the door before addressing the person behind it.

"Come in, Doctor," Farnsworth said.

Strickler entered, pausing when he saw the opulence of the room. It wasn't just better, it was purposefully better, as if Farnsworth had replaced every item, every fixture, to ensure that there were no similarities between where he laid his head and the men on the floor beneath him.

"Quit gawking, Ted," he said. "A closed mouth gathers no flies."

"How'd you know it was me?"

"It wasn't that difficult. You're the only one who hasn't sought me out alone yet. And you're the only one who could mask his true intentions behind the façade of a physician's concern. Now, what is it you wanted to ask me?"

Strickler fought the redness beginning to burn his cheeks. He walked around the room, evading Farnsworth's scrutiny until that insecure feeling passed. He picked up one of the tan prescription bottles off the night table and read it.

"May cause lightheadedness, blurred visions, delusions." He looked up at Farnsworth. "This is Phalomine. I've read about this. I didn't think the FDA approved this yet."

"It hasn't."

"This is no ulcer, Neal," Strickler said, as he put down the bottle.

"I'm so happy to see that Harvard Medical School hasn't dropped its reading standards. But I digress. I'm sure you didn't come up all these steps to just see about what pills I'm taking and when."

Strickler felt the heat rise again in his cheeks. Instead of deflecting the remark, he took another approach and embraced it.

"Neal, I wouldn't have come to you unless the situation warranted it."

"Money," Farnsworth said. "Everyone's favorite five-letter word."

"Yes, money, dammit! Sarah took me to the cleaners in the divorce."

"You can't blame her for the loss of your practice, Teddy-boy. She didn't make those business decisions. She didn't tell you to get high on your own supply. And she certainly didn't tell you to dip into her family's account."

Strickler was visibly flustered.

"I don't know what you're talking about."

"Which part? The prescription drug abuse? Or the fact that your sticky fingers dipped deeply into the family cookie jar?"

Strickler walked around the bed, standing beside the desk next to Farnsworth. Out of the corner of his eye, he glimpsed the heading of a page mostly covered by a manila folder. It read, *Last Will and Testament*."

"Look," he said. "This isn't looking for a leg-up like the others. A lot of good can come from this, Neal. For other people. Sick people. People that need help."

"And yourself."

"Yes, but that's not the motivation behind this. I'll pay the money back, Neal, with interest. It's not a hand-out. Consider it a loan, or an investment, if that better suits your sensibilities."

Farnsworth folded the newspaper in his hands and set it aside.

"When I was ten, my mother said I had such a serious look about me that I was either going to change the world or go insane trying to do so. I wonder what she would think of me now?"

Strickler went all in. He completely lowered his guard hoping that by showing vulnerability, Farnsworth would show compassion. That was a mistake he couldn't stop himself from making.

"Neal, I don't like doing this. You know that. Coming to you. Begging like I am. But I'm doing just that, Neal. I'm begging you. They took my house, Neal. They took my Goddamn house and my practice and my…my dignity."

"That's the rub. That's the thing. You know what the only real advantage of money is? It makes you stop worrying about money."

"That's not an answer."

"I invited all of you here to play a game. A simple game for which the winner will be compensated with hundreds of thousands of dollars. *One million*. And here you all are still asking for money. Go away, Ted. Finish the game. Win your way out of your situation."

Farnsworth dismissed Strickler by picking up the paper and opening it. The doctor turned and marched out of the room, slamming the door behind him.

Chapter 7

At ten minutes to eight, the three men assembled outside for the start of the evening's game. Farnsworth stood in front of them, handing them each a cell phone and a handheld Coleman lantern.

"Gentlemen, losers spend their lives thinking about what they're going to do. They never enjoy doing what they're doing. I'd say, let that be a lesson to you, but I think we can all agree that ship has long since sailed."

Farnsworth put a lantern in Strickler's hand.

"A lantern?"

"Excellent observation, Ted," Michaels said. "You never told us you got a degree for stating the obvious."

Farnsworth looked over at Michaels and raised his eyebrows in compliment to the insult. He turned back to Strickler and smiled.

"Ah, but when I am older, and am to do what I'm to do, O'Leerie I'll run around the night and light the lamps with you."

"Donne?" Chance inquired.

"Stevenson," Farnsworth corrected. "Find the fire that lights the lamp. That's all you have to do."

"I don't know about the rest of you," Chance said. "But I'm ready to redeem myself."

Farnsworth's face grew very serious. He stood in front of his friend, searching his eyes.

"Do you really believe that redemption is that easily obtained, Ethan?"

Chance squirmed under Farnsworth's gaze.

"It's just a saying."

"I think we all better hope that it is."

Zeke stepped up from the shadows.

"The van's ready, Mr. Farnsworth."

"Thank you, Zeke." Farnsworth turned his attention to the men. "I considered your suggestion from the previous night. Each of you now has a cell phone. Call the number on back to let Zeke you've completed the task at hand, and he'll bring you here. Any questions, campers?"

There are none.

"Let the game begin."

*****

Even though the township didn't seem that big, Zeke – or was it Farnsworth's call? – found the most remote places in town to drop them off. In Chance's case, he stood in a deserted, ugly section of town, what would be considered an "industrial" section of this little hamlet. A chain link fence surrounded a junk yard and what looked to be a small tool & die facility of some sort. One thing was certain; the place he was to find the flame to light this lamp was not going to be found here.

Chance gained his bearings. In his experience, locations like junkyards and factories were placed on the outskirts of a town, right at the edge and far removed from the sight of regular citizenry. Armed with that knowledge, he only had one choice: take the long road ahead of him to get back to where the clue would ultimately be found.

As he walked in that direction, he thought about what Michaels had said regarding Farnsworth's penchant for creating the dramatic. If that was true, it put everything that they were doing into a different light. Maybe there wouldn't be any windfall of money at the end of this shit-show tunnel. Maybe this was just Farnsworth being Farnsworth. Maybe he was just taking advantage of one more time to make his minions jump through the hoops he created for them. They still had to play the roles that they were given. The one-million-dollar tease assured Farnsworth of their cooperation. To not deliver that at the end was something that – well – Farnsworth would do.

That thought made his blood boil.

Too much was on the line for him to think that way.

He could not go back to Tom and write porn movies or be the subject of Tom's handheld camera amateur scenes. Tom assured him that it was only for his entertainment, something to watch by himself when his wife was away and Chance was not with him. But he didn't believe Tom any more than he believed he was going to show his father-in-law *The Sorrow Man*.

There was a time that he thought he could commit suicide. He was so sure of it that the idea of ending his life didn't scare him. He was very rational about it, taking the morning to brainstorm the ways he could kill himself, listing the pros and cons of each method, including things like clean up and body discovery. Committing such an act didn't have to be completely selfish. He did not want his success to be at the expense of some poor bystander or maid who might not be able to un-see a dead body in a state of gore or decay.

While almost benign, an overdose was not an advisable course of action. Too many times, people failed in the effort, often throwing up or waking up hours later alive and emotionally and physically drained. Shooting himself was completely out of the question. He had read about incidents where the person had second thoughts at the moment of trigger depression, moving the barrel slightly, and taking off the top of their head or blowing out their lower jaw.

After six hours of the most cogent, lucid thought he ever had, Chance realized that he simply wouldn't be able to do it. Even when he threw out post-death clean up concerns, he realized he simply didn't have it in him. So, he decided on the next best thing. He'd go into the shady parts of town and get robbed. He'd fight off the attacker, or pretend to, and get shot or knifed in the process. He'd become a quiet suicide – a crime statistic, a burglary gone bad. He walked up and down the spot known as the "Sugar Zone" one night but succeeded in only seeing how the street drug trade worked. No matter who he followed or stared at, he could not elicit the violent attention which he sought.

Even death proved too impossible to achieve for someone as unlucky as he was, a more depressing realization than the life he was leading. His existence was that disappointing.

As Chance approached the opening of a backstreet, he heard loud grunting; someone was in pain or causing it. It was a feral, almost bestial sound of someone or something caught in the trap. And like an accident along the side of the road, there was something compelling the passer-by to see it rather than turn away.

Chance slowly entered. The darkness was too thick to make out anything but heavy shadow, and he needed to get closer to see the cause of this primal condition. As he did the image became more discernible. So too did the smell. He gagged, fighting back the urge to puke, the odor of unwashed bodies and human feces welling up in his nasal passages.

Concealed behind a green dumpster, two bums coupled with the fervor of horny teenagers. The one on his knees turned to look back when he heard Chance's gag reflex.

"Who the hell are you?" he barked. The top didn't break rhythm and remained focused at the task at hand.

Chance stared for a moment, before uttering an apology.

"Sorry," he said but it was muffled as he choked back rising vomit.

"Get out of here, or join," the bottom yelled. "It's like you haven't seen a guy get fucked in the ass."

Horrified, Chance backed away and took off running with the sound of the bum's laughter ringing in his ears.

*****

Michaels moseyed down the street, half-singing, half-humming to himself, like a tippler without any set destination in mind. He paused by a streetlamp, taking advantage of the light to find his cigarettes and light one. He inhaled deeply looking up at the starry night. Damn, the sky was so clear in the country. He couldn't remember the last time he saw so many stars in the sky. Maybe as a kid at summer camp. But then he was too busy sneaking cigarettes and whatever alcohol could be pilfered from the counselors' lockers.

Speaking of which.

Michaels dipped into his back pocket and produced the flask that he had found in his room. He opened it and took a swig.

He started to hum a Door's tune. God, he liked to drink. He really had the taste for it. Drugs became less of a thing with him once he left college. He still smoked marijuana occasionally, but it wasn't the mainstay that it used to be. Working nine-to-five curbed him of that, especially as companies were adopting a no-tolerance policy of recreational drug consumption, despite some states becoming more lenient where that magic herb was concerned.

Michaels buzzed happily. It was reassuring feeling, one that he had sorely missed for the last five days. He earned the right for a cocktail or two, or at least that's what he told himself. He paused by a shop window and stared at his reflection. It was like looking at his own personal rendition of a Frankenstein. The pieces of his appearance were cobbled together from various odds and ends taken from other people, other sources. The face was familiar but everything else was different – the clothes, the lantern, the flask, the town.

Like all Frankensteins, Michaels needed to kill his creator.

That's what he told himself anyway but knew that was the booze talking. Still, he would be lying if he hadn't thought of offing Farnsworth. Hell, there wasn't a day in college that passed when he didn't want to push him in front of a bus or smother him in the next room while he slept. In the beginning, after several instances in which Farnsworth tore him down in front of other people, including the girl he had just started to date and whom Farnsworth fucked, Michaels kept a ledger of all his slights. He had filled two notebooks by the end of his junior year and ended up tossing them away. What had started as keeping a record of misdeeds became a thorn in Michaels' side, a painful reminder of just how inept he was at sticking up for himself.

It was easier to drink and smoke. And it certainly worked.

Look at him now.

Michaels looked at the flask in his hand, and immediately cursed himself for his weakness. He needed to figure out the clue, not get shit-faced drunk.

Michaels tucked the flask in his back-pocket moments before Strickler came up on him, emerging from a small park like lost dog.

"Sheriff sees you like that and you're liable to be arrested for intent," he said, as he walked past Michaels.

"Ted, you dropped something."

Strickler turned. Michaels smiled, and from behind his back with one hand, he pulled out his middle finger.

Strickler sighed, shook his head, and walked off.

*****

Michaels was such a prick, Strickler thought to himself as he trudged down the street. Of everyone re-assembled for this fantasy fiasco, he probably hated Michaels the most, maybe even more than Farnsworth, although that was debatable. Where Farnsworth was manipulative and devious, Michaels was just plain offensive. In college, his slacker lifestyle was corrosive – his appearance was slovenly, his personality was as compelling as a sloth's, and his manners were nonexistent. He was the epitome of everything Strickler abhorred, which was undoubtedly why Farnsworth made them live together. In their off-campus apartment, Farnsworth selected Chance to room with, dictating that the other bedroom to be shared by Michaels and Strickler. It was a deliberate decision, Farnsworth's way of telling Strickler that even though they might share a similar socio-economic background, they were not, and never would be, equals.

Despite his superiority in all things human, there was one thing that Michaels had over him, something that even though Michaels never mentioned, Strickler believed that his roomie lorded over him.

The two had made a private bet, a wager that they kept from Chance and Farnsworth. Even though these two detested each other, they could agree that such a wager was best made without any oversight from the resident dictator.

The Medical College Admission, or MCAT, was designed to help medical schools test and evaluate the most qualified among a vast pool of aspirants. One did not go to medical school without passing this test and passing it with high marks. The bet was simple; whoever got the highest mark had bragging rights – albeit in private – over the other. During an argument over something that Strickler had long since forgotten, the two made the bet and set the criteria.

Back then, the overall MCAT score was based on six sections being scored on a 15-point scale. When the grades came back, Michaels had edged Strickler by five points. Five points. Strickler went crazy. He stormed out of the campus pub where the two had met to show their results and ended spending the night at the local motel at the base of the hill. Strickler managed to successfully parry Farnsworth's inquisition as to his whereabouts by saying his father had made an impromptu visit, and after a late dinner, had decided to spend the night in the motel. Farnsworth's suspicions were acquiesced by Michael's corroboration. In Farnsworth's estimation, Michaels would willingly give up Strickler on a lie than corroborate one, and he ultimately accepted it as such.

If there was a God, a lightning strike would hit Farnsworth and Michaels with one shot, sort of a two-for-one deal.

But wishing bad things wasn't enough. Sometimes it needed a hand to nudge it in the right direction.

Sometimes, even God needed a little help.

Attrition

*****

The East Bumfuck Volunteer Fire Department was a small group of local professionals that worked regular day jobs in addition to serving in the town's cadre of "bravest" unpaid civil servants. Two firemen sat out front on a bench taking in the evening. One was an older man with a slight paunch doing a crossword puzzle. Pharmacist by day, he was the lieutenant of this crew of bona-fide heroes by night. He looked every part the veteran with a salt and pepper walrus moustache that practically buried his mouth in facial hair. Next to him, a very clean-shaven young recruit read a copy of a tabloid magazine. Barely out of high school, his only meaningful employment was delivering hardware supplies for his father's store when not waiting for something to happen when on call.

"You think she's hot?" the young recruit asked his mentor. He showed him a picture of a medically enhanced blonde in a skimpy bikini.

"Sure," said the older man, more concerned with his crossword than on an over-glossed air-brushed photo.

"I don't think her tits are real."

"No kidding. What gave it away?"

From the end of the block, Chance saw the two firemen out front. He looked at the lantern in his hand. Suddenly, a metaphoric lightbulb went off above his head. He hustled over to the two men.

"Excuse me, officers," he said.

Neither recruit nor grizzled veteran looked up from their respective magazines.

"We ain't the police, buddy," the veteran said, penciling in the answer to *Gone With the Wind's famous home*. "What do you want?"

"I'm here for the fire," Chance said.

"Fire? What fire?" the recruit looked up at Chance, now interested.

"We didn't get any fire call, mister," the veteran sighed, trying to rein in his enthusiastic but intellectually-challenged recruit.

"No, I'm sorry," Chance said and held up the Coleman lantern. "I mean this. Fire, get it? I need the fire to go in there."

Puzzled, the recruit looked over at the veteran. The older man squinted at Chance.

"Are you funning with us? You high on something?"

"What? No, I was..."

"We're first responders. We take care of people. This isn't a joke. Where you from? You aren't from around here, are you?"

"I was just trying to find something to light this." Chance held up the lantern.

The veteran shared an incredulous look with the recruit.

"You're nuts and this ain't the looney house. You got a lantern? You need kerosene. No kerosene, no flame. That's the way it works, shit-for-brains."

"Kerosene," Chance said in a moment of enlightenment. "Thanks!"

"Beat it, numbskull," the vet said.

*****

Shay's Department Store's dim security lights could barely be seen from the street. It was one of the largest buildings in town, two stories tall and occupying a full block. Michaels smoked a cigarette, watching the front as a deputy's car rolled by. He wasn't going to risk a second encounter with East Bumfuck's finest. Last night he could have explained away as an anomaly. Being caught a second time "casing" a storefront for the sake of playing a game would be far too much for anyone to believe.

Once the car turned the corner and was out of sight, Michaels made his move. He shuffled quickly across the street, taking the time to make sure there were no other bystanders around. He didn't want to happen upon someone walking dogs or going out for a stroll to take in the night air, or whatever reason any of the town's residents might be outside of their residences at this hour.

Satisfied he was alone, Michaels turned his attention to the store's window. He pressed his face against the glass, cupping his hands around his eyes to get a better view inside. The front of this rural cornucopia featured accessories of all kinds – perfumes, colognes, and what looked to be a discount and sales rack. More stuff was in back and he could see a pair of escalators that brought customers to an upper and basement level.

Michaels looked around for something to get him inside the store. A survey of the street revealed nothing useful, save for a loose brick from the curb. He picked up the brick and checked the weight in his hand. He wasn't sure if it would smash the window glass, but maybe just heavy enough to get through the pane in the door. He rapped it lightly. If he smashed it hard enough, it would give. Michaels readied his arm, taking a few deep breaths. He'd have to get inside as quickly as possible and have no more than few minutes to find the clue, write his name, and get the hell out of Dodge.

Michaels grabbed the door handle to steady the door when something unexpected happened. It depressed easily and the front door opened. It was unlocked.

Michaels smiled. He set the brick aside, happily dodging a potential pitfall. He went inside, closing the door behind him.

He clicked the penlight on, moving the small beam around the immediate vicinity. He felt small in the large room, and the farther he walked in, the more he felt like he was slipping deeper down the throat of a large, ravenous mouth. He looked around for something that would serve as a light to the Coleman lantern. He didn't think that department stores had a section that sold cigarettes and cigars, so where would one find a lighter?

He passed through the women's section and into men's apparel. He brushed past trousers and sport coats, the metal hangars twinkling musically like wind chimes. Even though he was alone and any security alarm – if one existed – was obviously turned off, he tried to move as quietly as possible. There was a certain peace that settled in the hours after customers had spent the day intruding on the goods, fingering items with a consumer callousness. After being manhandled, clothes had been refolded and tucked neatly back into order.

Now he moved past jewelry...past accessories...past the perfume and colognes. Eventually, Michaels found himself standing in front of the escalators. He smiled at the metaphor – to go up or down? To go to heaven, or be regulated to hell?

Michaels instinctively took the escalator down. He didn't know why. It just felt right.

The bottom floor featured outdoor goods. He wasn't surprised that the entire basement was dedicated to the sporting life. East Bumfuck was what you expected in a region like this where flannel was king, and people usually had more than one fishing rod and shotgun.

The penlight beam coursed over tackle boxes, fishing and hunting knives, a locked case featuring hunting rifles of various calibers, knapsacks and cast-iron cooking equipment.

As Michaels pressed further on, his movement set off a motion detector light that brightly lit up a mannequin display.

It depicted a family camping scene. The center piece was a dome-style four-season red tent with a front flap supported by two tent poles. A mother was positioned over a makeshift fire, positioned to grab a kettle of coffee. The father mannequin sat in a canvas folding chair, staring out at a cardboard blue lake.

Behind them, unnoticed by the parents, perhaps even ignored, was a smaller mannequin of a young woman, presumably their daughter, maybe fifteen or sixteen years old.

But what was disturbing was how she was positioned.

On her knees, the girl mannequin had her arms thrust upward and crossed, as if trying to fend off or defend an attack from an unseen, horrifying threat. What's more, was the expression on the all-too-real mannequin's face– complete horror, eyes wide, and mouth frozen open in silent scream.

Michaels didn't move. He couldn't move. The face was so lifelike, so very much real, that his stomach jolted. He barely made it to a metal cooking pot before he evacuated his stomach inside the black cast iron cookware. After three violent heaves, he stood up wiping his mouth with the back of his hand.

Next to the circle of rocks that formed the fire, was Farnsworth's message spelled out in rocks:

"Good job campers, object number two found..."

"You sick fuck," Michaels said, as he leaned over and spelled out his initials with a pile of stones.

*****

Outside, Strickler waited for Michaels to exit Shay's Department Store before he made his presence known. Michaels had been a while inside and didn't appear in too much of a hurry to find an alternative location. This had to be it.

Strickler waited until Michaels had turned the corner before he stepped out of shadows across the street. He didn't need more smug remarks from Michaels. He could accept the fact that he was shadowing Michaels as he searched for the clue. He justified it as working smarter instead of harder, instead of acknowledging his inability to decipher the clues set forth before them. His mind didn't work that way, and he didn't want to accept that as a simple left-brain/right-brain reality. Michaels somehow did both; admitting that he leaned one way would mean Michaels was somehow superior to him, and that would never, ever happen.

Once Michaels was out of sight, Strickler made sure the coast was clear and went inside the store.

*****

Strickler's face remained impassive when he saw the mannequin display. As a surgeon, he'd seen his share of blood and trauma. He had overheard patients pray and whisper their fears and anxieties to their loved ones in the time leading up to life-or-death surgeries. He had even informed families and next of kin that their son, husband, father, mother, sister did not make it, their bodies too weak to survive medicine's intervention. He watched their faces when he delivered the news, saw how hopeful expectation drained from their eyes as if a stop had been removed. He had never felt sympathy or empathy for these people. It was simple biology, and biology, like nature, always emerged on top.

But this was different. There was an intimation being expressed here – the architect of this life-size diorama wanted to elicit a specific reaction from his audience. This was a perversion of the normal, what he imagined sociological experimentation or performance art to be. Although he never had played a game manufactured by Farnsworth Enterprises, if this was sample of what they produced, Strickler was glad he had never wasted the time or money.

Calmly, Stricker walked over where Michaels had written his initials. The doctor took some of the stones from Michaels' initials and used them with others to write his name in bigger letters.

*****

Tears rolled down Chance's cheeks. Standing before the mannequin display was like standing before something moving at a museum. Whether it was an object, a piece of art, a photograph, the best pieces made the viewer feel something, experience something. And Chance was feeling something. Loss? Fear? Solitude? Some fusion of all three?

The more he looked, the more Chance knew this was not art.

While Chance was no stranger to crying, the tears that he shed were typically in response to a specific condition or situation. He cried because he was in pain, especially when Tom used those "toys" on him. He cried when his frustration was so insurmountable and overwhelming that it literally consumed him until it spit him out. He cried when there was a sliver of hope, a taunting glimmer of a promise that could be. When it came to other things like death, he was more ambivalent. When he was boy around eleven, in one December now known as "Black Christmas", he had three close family members die within a span of two weeks – his grandfather, his aunt, and his sister. By the time he saw his sister in the coffin at the wake, he had used up all his tears. He had simply none left to give.

This girl, this mannequin, touched him in the way that few things did of this nature. He knew that expression because he had worn it on several occasions. Maybe not outwardly, but internally, and privately. Many times, the face that he showed the world was not the one that he kept protected deep down.

No, he thought to himself. This wasn't like visiting an art museum at all.

This was more like what he felt when he saw the Holocaust Museum for the first time.

The tears continued to come even as Chance took the remaining stones and placed them near those of his friends.

*****

The three men waited in front of the East Bumfuck Church. They were silent, preferring quiet introspection to engaging in talk. It was evident that they had all seen firsthand the latest clue, and that no one need to discuss how twisted it was. Silence was confirmation enough.

When Zeke pulled up the van, they all got inside. He looked at their faces in the rearview mirror.

"Y'all find it?" he asked them.

They answered in short nods or murmured responses.

"Figured you'd be happy about it," Zeke snorted, then started the van up and drove down the road. They had finished early. It was only ten-thirty.

*****

Rachmaninoff's "Isle of the Dead" played from the speakers in Farnsworth's room. He stood by the window, waiting for the headlights to appear in the distance. When he saw them finally approach, he watched carefully as it parked, looking intently at the faces of his three friends when they climbed out and passed under the lights of the front porch.

They moved slowly, and in single file, each face more somber than the last. It reminded him of condemned people walking up the gallows to their execution.

Farnsworth smiled, letting himself enjoy the feeling of a job well done.

*****

Later that evening, Farnsworth drew himself a hot bath and sank his body into the forgiving water. His body was slowly betraying him bit by bit and he needed every bit of the opiates to get him over the hump. Knowing that he was dying didn't depress Farnsworth; he had done everything important that he had set out to accomplish. When Deborah was alive, he had struggled to get more time to invest into his commercial endeavors and aspirations. He'd barter with his wife, though she was a shrewd negotiator. Even when Farnsworth thought he had "won" an argument, he soon found out it was a strategic play by his wife which ended up pulling him from work to enjoy life outside the office. Once Deborah passed, there was only work to concentrate on and fill those empty hours, but the interest had subsided. Success was nothing if there wasn't someone with which to share it.

Farnsworth grabbed the thick tumbler of scotch and took a sip. It didn't go down as smoothly as it had before the disease took firmer hold, but he didn't care. He was going to drink it until the bottle of his own life ran dry.

While Farnsworth ruminated on the past in the bathroom, the bedroom door opened and a figure – *somebody* – walked quietly inside, making the sure the door closed without a sound. The Figure looked around the opulent room. A nearby clock read a quarter after twelve. Farnsworth was nowhere in sight.

The Figure was about to leave when he heard the unmistakable splash of water coming from the bathroom. Then it turned to see the light underneath the closed door.

Farnsworth did not immediately look up from his drink when the bathroom door opened. When he did, he seemed unsurprised at the person in front of him. He took another drink, resting the glass on the edge of the tub.

"Feel free to come in," he said to the Figure who remained standing in front of him. Farnsworth neither looked surprised nor afraid.

The Figure did not respond.

"I was wondering which of you would come here first. But I have to admit, I never thought it would be you. I guess I shouldn't be totally surprised. I've always underestimated you, haven't I?"

Again, no response came from the Figure. Farnsworth motioned to the radio perched on the toilet seat next to the bath.

"Would you mind turning that up a bit? Rachmaninoff. He was really experimenting with orchestration at this point in his career. This is where he really found his own voice. So dark and dreamlike, don't you think?"

The Figure did not respond. A gloved hand reached out and turned up the music, but then lingered on the radio.

Farnsworth noticed the Figure lift the radio off the toilet, turning it over, inspecting it. If he was scared, he didn't show it. He grabbed the glass and downed the scotch in one gulp, holding the burning sensation in his mouth for as long as he could before swallowing it all down. Then he slid further down into the tub, getting himself more comfortable.

"You know why I like baths so much? No matter where you've been or what you've done, it's the only one place where you can feel truly clean. All the dirt, all the grime in the hard to reach places, just lifts off your body and settles on the top."

The Figure released the plugged-in radio into the full bathtub. Any light that was on now violently flickered, casting extreme and twisted shadows in quick bursts. Farnsworth's body convulsed in the tub, jolts of electricity rippling through him. The entire time his pale blue eyes stared at the Figure – no resentment, no anger – just a contentment born from knowing that it was all, finally, over.

Chapter 8

Michaels called his wife again. It was the eighth time in two hours. Each time he was met with the house answering machine, a throw-back piece of equipment in a time when technology was getting smarter, smaller, and infinitely more expensive. The ninth time didn't go through at all – the machine was full.

Her cell phone did not yield any more favorable results.

He hung up and sat on his bed, thinking. Where could she be? It wasn't like his wife not to be at home. Her movements and whereabouts were never under question because she never veered from a routine that she had imposed on herself. Could she be out with a friend for dinner or drinks? Of course, but not at this hour. It was just past midnight.

Could she be having an affair to deliver some payback for Michaels' indiscretions? The answer was the same. Of course, but not at this hour. It was the time that made these possibilities, well, relatively impossible.

Suzy was in bed – their bed – no later than ten at night. Always. Since the day they were married until now. Besides, if she wanted to screw around on him, she had all day to do so and still be in bed by ten. That Michaels could believe and if he was being honest, was more in line with her character.

Complete radio silence wasn't.

Michaels made a few phone calls to some friends and family. Anyone he could get on the line told him the same thing – they hadn't heard from Suzy.

Finally, he called Gail Bernstein, the next-door neighbor. He could tell that he had woken her up but didn't feel bad about that.

"I'm sorry Gail," he said. "I know it's late, but I've been trying to get in touch with Suzy all night and she's not there. Have you seen her?"

Gail didn't immediately respond and sighed loudly. A sick feeling started to form in the center of Michaels' chest, an ice ball of insecurity.

"What is it, Gail?"

"I thought she would have told you this," she said. "She left, Bern'. She moved out today."

"What? Why?"

Another pause on Gail's end.

"Why do you think?" she asked. "Because of your...your...ways." She struggled to find a diplomatic term for his whoring appetite.

"Where'd she go? Did she leave a number? I have to speak to her, Gail. Some important things have come up, and I need to speak to her."

"She didn't tell me, Bernie. Honest. I'm sorry."

"Don't give me that shit, Gail. I'm serious."

"I'm sorry," she said again and hung up the phone.

Michaels called her right back, but she didn't respond. On the third time she had shut off her phone entirely.

"Fuck!" Michaels screamed, throwing his phone against the bed. He needed to talk to Suzy. He needed to get grounded and she always knew a way to bring him back when certain incidents made him go crazy. She was his point of light in an otherwise dark existence. Yeah, he went with other women. But only for sex. There was nothing else involved but penetration and release.

Without Suzy, there was only one option left for Michaels.

He retrieved the flask from his night table and opened it. He brought it to his lips and tilted his head back, trying to empty the contents into his stomach until the ice ball in his chest had melted.

*****

Strickler checked his messages. One after another, bad news piled up until there was little else. The second to last message informed him that the lawsuit had been initiated against him for malpractice. His license was suspended indefinitely pending the results of the lawsuit. The rest of his patients had given him notice of their departure from his practice. The last message was perhaps the hardest to hear – Mina, his long serving jack-of-all-trades had tendered her verbal resignation.

Strickler was not given to emotional outbursts. Even at a young age he didn't see the point in throwing a tantrum or storming up and down lamenting why he was not getting what he wanted. When other kids wailed to their parents, Strickler became more introspective, rethinking his approach to his parents – or as he did later – his teachers, to get what he wanted. This worked well into college until he crossed paths with Farnsworth. Then all his attempts of remaining stoic in times of adversity went down the tubes. Farnsworth hit all the right buttons, taking great personal enjoyment in being able break down Strickler's stern austerity and making him more like Michaels than he cared to admit to himself.

Now anything could set Stricker off. He had no patience when things didn't go his way. And while it was easy to work himself up, coming down was another issue entirely. He didn't find much comfort in alcohol. That was too simple of a sedative, a too easy fix for people who were weak in body and spirit.

Fentanyl on the other hand was another animal altogether. "China White" was a fitting slang term for the opiate since its potent affect put the user in a slumber that harkened memories of sailors wasting away in opium parlors in Southeast Asia. And right now, as Strickler checked his pulse rate against his wrist, he needed a contrast to what he was feeling.

He found his medical bag and dumped its contents on the bed. He found the packet of syringes and removed one from the sleeve. He then found the vial.

It had been a while since he last shot up. Considering all that happened, he figured he was due.

Even in his addiction, Strickler was methodical. He didn't overindulge, which would have been something Michaels would have done if given the chance. He measured just enough to chip at the anxiety building within him.

When he depressed the plunger, all that had happened in the past twenty-four hours would be carried away, if just for a little while.

*****

Chance's phone call did not go well. Tom was in one of his moods. He didn't want to tell him that he wouldn't be home at the time they had agreed upon, but what was he to do? The game wasn't done yet, and while he hoped that he would win the one million dollars, Chance didn't believe he could win. One thing was constant in his life – bad luck followed him around like toilet paper stuck to his shoe. And when he did try to remove it, his hand inevitably came up smelling like shit.

Chance thought about the game. It was odd to say the least, and not what he had expected it to be.

He had played a dinner murder mystery before. It was set during the roaring '20s at a speakeasy. Characters had kitschy names like "Hersh E. Bar" and "Mickey the Fish" and everyone had to dress up per the styles of the period. Truth be told, it was more campy than serious, and got sillier as Gin Rickeys and Sidecars were generously poured by waiters throughout the course of the evening.

This was an entirely different beast. The game – well, it didn't seem like much of a game, no matter how much Farnsworth tried to paint it otherwise. It was darker, mysterious yes, but everything – the nature of the game, how they had to go find the clues, how the clues were constructed – seemed more like he was trying to punish them, rather than reward them.

Chance shook his head. But not many games offered a one-million-dollar purse. So yeah, maybe Farnsworth was just being Farnsworth, getting them together for one more run through his "fuck you" team-building exercise, but he never welched on paying off what he said he would. And if history stood correct, he wouldn't here either.

He didn't want to go back to Tom. He didn't want that damn life. He couldn't take another minute doing those things with that man. He wasn't going to do it again. He had made some tough decisions and taken some drastic actions before; he'd do so again if he had to.

And with Tom, he might just have to.

Attrition

Farnsworth's lifeless body looked emaciated and lean, ravaged by the disease that broke him down internally. The Medical Examiner from the nearby town wrote notes about the scene while his assistant snapped photographs. Sheriff Waters stood at the door, letting the men do their work. He moved a toothpick around his mouth as he watched the medical professionals do their job.

Waters gestured to the smirk frozen on Farnsworth's death face.

"Fucking freaky, ain't it, Darrell? Corpses grinnin' at you like that. Like nothin's botherin' them and they got nothing but time. Almost like he ain't dead at all."

The assistant lowered his camera.

"He's dead alright, Sheriff," he said. "Deader than disco."

The M.E. finished scribbling and turned to the Sheriff.

"Hell, I once hauled a body out of his car wrecked after this hooker had been working on his jammie. Found him two days later. He had shit himself silly, but boy, the smile on that guy's face would have made a catfish proud."

"So, what are we looking at here, D? I got three city boys out there twitching something fierce. Does one of them got a problem?"

The intimation was clear, but the M.E. just shook his head.

"I'm not seeing it. The signs aren't there."

"People have a way of doctoring things to suit their narrative," the Sheriff suggested.

Again, the M.E. shook his head.

"I'll know more after a bit, but my gut instinct? This wasn't the result of any foul play. Well, at least not by outside forces."

"So, what are you saying? He offed himself?"

"Looks to be the case," the M.E. said. "I'll let you know if we dig up anything else."

"Good enough for me," Waters said. He walked out into Farnsworth's bedroom where Chance, Michaels, and Strickler stood next to the deputy Michaels ran from the previous night.

"What's the prognosis?" Strickler asked.

"We're conducting our initial investigations," Waters told him. He didn't like people that weren't from around the area. They came in flocks when the leaves turned colors, causing traffic jams and turning the normally nice, quiet town into their own amusement park. "Why don't you boys head on downstairs. This might take a while."

The three men looked at each other and did as they were instructed. When it came to Farnsworth, the unexpected was the one thing you could expect. And this just topped the expected "unexpected" list.

*****

The men sat in the dining room. Chance sipped a glass of sherry, constantly turning the cordial glass stem around in his hand. Strickler waited by the window, staring out as the morning sun had pushed into late afternoon. Michaels paced back and forth like a caged, agitated cat. Six hours had passed since they were initially dismissed from Farnsworth's quarters. They just sat around, waiting for the Sheriff to tell them what the hell had happened.

The deputy was finishing up an interview with Zeke in the other room. They had each been interviewed alone and provided their signed statements for the record. Zeke was the last, and having just met Farnsworth, had the briefest of interrogations.

Michaels stopped by the dining room wet bar. A drink would be good right now. Something that would settle the nerves and level him off. He was about to grab a bottle when Zeke sauntered into the room. He sat down across from Chance and stared at no one and nothing in particular.

Chance stood up.

"Can someone say something please? No one's spoken for hours."

"What do you want us to say?" Strickler asked.

"It doesn't matter. Anything. Our friend is dead from a horrible accident. A horrible, horrible accident."

"That was no accident," Strickler said.

"What do you mean? Of course, it was. Unless...are you saying that he killed himself?"

"I'm a doctor, not a detective. But come on, who puts a radio so close to a bathtub?"

"Oh God," Chance said. He sat back down. "Do you think he suffered?"

"Electrocution? Depends on how many volts run through your body. In some instances, you would go up in a snap; others, well, you would just slow cook like a rotisserie chicken."

"There's that bedside manner," Michaels said. He shrugged and reached for some bourbon and a glass and poured himself a very stiff drink. Appearances could go suck-it. Special circumstances required special privileges.

"Better give back that eighteen-month coin," Strickler said. "Another addict back at the trough."

"No," Michaels said thoughtfully. "Your mother went back to the trough. I was just there to give it to her."

"Such an asshole," Strickler hissed.

"Jesus," Chance said. "You two never stop. That's our friend up there or did you forget? Lying dead in a bath. A bath of all things..."

"You're right," Michaels said. "I always pictured him being gunned down or run over. But not in a bath."

Strickler snorted. "Sounds like you had it in for him," Strickler said.

Michaels downed his drink and poured himself another.

"Oh, right," he said, moving from the wet bar. "And none of you ever thought about it once. Please…"

Sheriff Waters entered the room. The men immediately broke from their line of conversation. He held their statements in his hand.

"Thank you, gentlemen, for your cooperation. I think I got all I needed here for now," he said.

Zeke got up from his seat. Waters waved him down.

"I'll see myself out, Zeke," he said.

"Suit yourself, Sheriff," the old man replied.

"You fellas stick around another day or so, will you? Would hate to have to call you back here for any follow up. You understand."

"Sure thing," Chance said. "Can you tell us what happened?"

The Sheriff shook his head. "Not tonight," the Sheriff said, and with that he left the room, leaving the four men there looking at one another.

*****

Marty Quinlan wore an expensive suit and sat in the living room drinking coffee when Michaels came down the steps. Chance and Strickler were already in the dining room eating breakfast. Michaels looked at the strange man, who was intently focused on reading the local newspaper. Neither one exchanged a greeting, although Quinlan lowered the paper to get a good look at the last of the persons stated in Farnsworth's will. Michaels went quickly to the kitchen and got himself some coffee.

None of them recognized him, Quinlan mused. It wasn't a surprise. Quinlan didn't usually socialize with underclassmen at college. Farnsworth was the exception. He had the charisma to draw you in and keep you in his sphere like a swirling eddy.

"Who's the suit?" Michaels asked when he sat down at the dining room table.

"I don't know," Chance said. "When I introduced myself, he just smiled politely at me and went back reading the paper."

"When do you think we can get out of here?" Strickler asked.

"Probably today at some point, I'd imagine," Chance replied.

"Great," Michaels said.

A moment of silence came over the trio before a thought occurred to Chance.

"What's going to happen to Farnsworth?"

"What do you mean?" Strickler asked.

"I mean his funeral arrangements. He didn't have any siblings. No children that I know of. And his wife…"

"I'm sure he had a will or something," Michaels said. "Someone will get him. I want to know what happens to the money."

"Maybe we can just split it?" Chance offered.

Strickler shook his head. "No, I don't think Farnsworth would have made it that easy for us."

"So, what are we supposed to do now?" Chance asked.

"We wait," Strickler said.

"Wait? For what?"

"For me."

The men turned. At the entrance of the dining room, the man in the fancy suit stood, a briefcase in hand.

"Who are you?" Michaels asked.

"Marty Quinlan," he said. "The lawyer."

*****

Zeke rolled a television with a DVD player into the dining room. The men sat in their seats. They were quietly watching the events unfold around them, unsure of what to make of what was happening.

"Thank you, Zeke," the lawyer said. He opened his briefcase, withdrew a DVD, and put it in the player and pressed "start." He watched the attentive looks on the men's faces as the video's image suddenly jumped to life.

On screen, they were met with the back of a brown leather high-backed chair that suddenly spun around to reveal Farnsworth with that customary cocky smirk on his face. He started laughing robustly.

"I wish you could see the looks on your faces. Well, I wish I could see them for that matter, but I know they must be doozies. Come on boys, close your mouths. It's like you haven't seen a ghost before. Boo!"

The men exchanged looks. This was weird even by Farnsworth's standards.

"Is this a joke?" Chance asked, turning to the lawyer.

"Please, just watch the video," Quinlan directed.

On screen, Farnsworth got more serious, dropping any hint of humor from his face. He stared intently at the men who were watching him.

"If you're watching this, that means I've passed onto the next world. Let's hope for my sake, it's a trip up and not down."

Farnsworth got up from his seat and stretched. He grabbed the cane off the floor and walked over to the bar and fixed himself a drink. He was taking his time. His motions were deliberate. These were his final words on earth, and he was going to have them his way without interference or interruption. He sipped his drink, staring at the camera, which made it look like he was staring right at the men with his cold, judging eyes. After a long pause, he began to speak again.

"When you occupy a cherished slot in the Fortune 500, I think you can safely assume that you have amassed nothing short of a small fortune. Cars, houses, planes…you have these things. They become less luxury items and more trappings that are expected of the upper one percent of the U.S. population, don't you think?"

Strickler made a face. Farnsworth was such an arrogant asshole.

"Anyway," Farnsworth continued, "Deborah and I never had children. We tried several times. We even discussed using medicine to help us conceive, but we both agreed that children are God's prerogative, not ours. If we couldn't have kids naturally, we took it as a sign that we were not meant to have them. Which lead me to a question – without a sired heir, what does a person do with a net worth conservatively estimated at eight billion dollars?"

The dining room was deathly silent, an appropriate mood for the gathering. There was no masking the men's surprise. They knew he was rich, but not *that* rich.

Farnsworth picked lint off the pocket of his light blue button-down oxford shirt.

"I know what you're thinking – donate it to worthy cause. Some would say, help humanity, Farnsworth. There are needy people, Farnsworth. You have so much money, Farnsworth. Spread it around…Well, I say, 'fuck 'em.' Those people are the same opportunists who veil their ineptitude and try to promote their value under the guise of selfless acts…who have never worked for anything in their miserable lives…who never understood the meaning of desire and achievement."

Farnsworth killed his drink with one gulp without any adverse facial reaction. A statement.

"No, theatrical altruistic grandstanding aside, there is only one true way to divide a kingdom. You give it to one king. And that's what I'm going to do. So, scholars, as of this moment, the one million dollars is officially off the table. The stakes are now raised, and the bar set so much higher. Winner take all is the new deal. Let me repeat that so there's no misunderstanding: winner take all. There is no second or third place and the winner will be legally compelled to keep the money or risk forfeiture. I'll let that sink in for a few moments."

Farnsworth kept his unblinking stare fixed at the faces he could not see but knew would be looking at him.

Quinlan paused the DVD. He turned to the men who all sat uncomfortably in their seats. They didn't meet his gaze; they couldn't. How else was one catch supposed his breath in the middle of an avalanche?

"I need a verbal agreement from all of you now. If you aren't willing to subscribe to this proposition, then you must vacate the room now."

Quinlan allowed ample time for each man to take-in the information, digest it, and come to some conclusion. One by one, they nodded their heads.

"I'm sorry gentlemen, but that won't do. I'll need a verbal confirmation."

"Yes," Strickler said.

"Yeah," Michaels said.

"Of course," Chance said.

With that, Quinlan started the DVD again. The stagnant image of Farnworth twitched to life.

"What can I say," he said. "I've had a good run. I've literally accomplished every single professional goal I laid out for myself once I left those hallowed halls of our higher education institution. I've lived enough for six lifetimes, no less one. I make no apologies for what I've done or who I am. Could there have been things I've done better? Sure. No question. But I did what I did and how it falls out in the end is not for me to judge."

Farnsworth looked at something off camera. A wistful smile crossed his face. He held it for a few seconds. When he turned back to the camera, the smile was gone and replaced by those hard, calculating eyes.

"But I'll let you all in on a little secret. The thing I'm going to miss most in the afterworld? It's not people. It's not things. It's not money...No, the thing I'm going to miss most is what money makes people do."

He smirked and winked at the camera. The television screen suddenly stopped, replaced by the light blue of DVD's end.

Quinlan turned off the television. He retrieved his briefcase from the floor and set it at on the dining room table. He clicked it open as he addressed the men. Michaels was the first one to speak.

"Was that real?" he said.

"Is it even legal?" Chance offered.

Quinlan interjected quickly and definitively.

"My assurances, Mr. Chance. It is. Mr. Farnsworth and I drew up the papers weeks ago. And let me assure you now as I assured him then. Everything's legal and binding."

The lawyer removed three thick copies of a contract for each man to sign. He passed them to Chance who passed them out to Michaels and Strickler.

"It's a weighty document before you now," Quinlan continued. "Let me present you the brass tacks. The offer is simple and non-negotiable – continue to play and finish the game. Whoever solves the mystery becomes sole beneficiary of Farnsworth Enterprises."

He let that reality sink in.

"Jesus Christ," Michaels said finally. He shook his head in disbelief.

"He has nothing to do with this," Strickler said. He grabbed a pen and started initialing pages.

"Two conditions must first be met. They are very strict and if not followed to the letter, also risk forfeiture of the Farnsworth estate."

"And these are?" Strickler asked.

"One, the game must be finished at all costs. Same rules will apply as they did when Farnsworth was monitoring activities. I will provide the final two clues, but the game must be played to its inevitable conclusion. There is no bowing out."

"Agreed, what's the second?" Chance asked.

And here Quinlan smiled. It reminded Michaels of the way a lizard's lips might look if it tried to smile.

"It's not so much a condition as a piece of information. A critical piece of information that will propel you on toward your goal. However, I can't impart that to you until all contracts are initial and signed."

Strickler put down his pen.

"Look, I may not be a muckity-muck attorney, but even I know not to sign anything without knowing what's behind door number two."

"He has a point," Chance said, pausing his own signing. "Signing blind is crazy. You wouldn't tell your clients to do that."

"You're right. I wouldn't. But none of my clients ever had the opportunity to possess eight billion dollars for playing a game. Remarkable circumstances require remarkable actions."

He saw that the men were not one hundred percent on board.

"Gentlemen," Quinlan said. "Everything can end right here. All you have to do is walk away and pick up your lives right where you left them. You leave with what you came with and that includes any hope you had of something better."

Quinlan removed additional files from the briefcase. One for each of the men. He started with Michaels.

"Mr. Michaels," he said in an accusatory tone. "A degenerate addictive personality, you have overindulged in vices and committed a series of infidelities."

"Now wait a second…" Michaels started but stopped when he realized that Quinlan wasn't stopping him.

"You squandered your daughter's college fund after you invested in a failed start-up, correct?"

Michaels said nothing but turned away, helping himself to more bourbon.

Quinlan picked up a second file and opened it.

"Dr. Strickler, you lost the majority of your private practice through a combination of impropriety and an unhealthy appetite for opiates," Quinlan said. "Perhaps more damning is liberally helping yourself to your wife's private family account without her knowledge or permission."

Strickler's face flushed a deep scarlet red.

"That's a damn lie! I'll sue you for defamation and libel!"

Nonplussed, Quinlan picked up the third file. Chance closed his eyes.

"No, please don't..."

"Mr. Chance spent six months homeless turning tricks to not-so-generous men in exchange for money, shelter, and in those rare instances when he had none, food."

Chance buried his face in his hands. The three of them sat there, humiliated as their dirty laundry was aired before everyone.

"If I may," Quinlan continued. "That's why you wear the particular regalia you do. Each one depicts the representations of someone else's ugly secret."

He nodded to Chance. "You represent Michaels' slovenly hedonistic appetites."

To Michaels, he said, "You, the thieving tendencies of Dr. Strickler."

To Strickler, he said, "A street whore turning tricks. What Mr. Chance might refer to as a 'chicken hawk'."

"These were jokes, albeit cruel, at your expense for someone of Mr. Farnsworth's dark sense of humor. As I've said, there are no consolation prizes. There are no parting gifts. Or you can enjoy another two days away from these... troubles."

The men looked like the very air was sucked from their lungs. There was no fight or defiance in their eyes. Any swagger, any pride, any defiance, had long since been beaten down under the attorney's relentless cross-examination.

"So, gentlemen, do you sign the contracts before or do you each walk out of here wiser but infinitely poorer? You have five minutes to decide before this offer will be rescinded."

The men look at one another. They all knew that they were all going to say yes but were waiting on for one to make the first move.

"I'm in," Strickler said.

"Me too," Michaels contributed.

"In for a penny...," Chance said, his voice trailing off.

Quinlan smiled as each man initialed and signed the pages before him. Quinlan took the time to review each to ensure that nothing underhanded had transpired, that each man's signature was correct and legal, and that all pages contained the same initials. Once he was satisfied that the task had been accomplished, he collected each and put them into his briefcase and locked it.

"Excellent, gentlemen. Until tonight then."

Quinlan prepared to leave when Chance raised a final question.

"Wait a second. What's the second condition? What's that piece of information?"

The lawyer looked at Chance with a disapproving eye.

"Isn't it obvious? Farnsworth did not commit suicide. He was murdered."

Chapter 9

The men congregated on the front porch, away from the lawyer. Michaels lit a cigarette, handing it to Chance before lighting himself one. The lawyer's words still lingered on the three men like a heavy cologne. Murder was a word that most people did not use lightly, and when said, cast suspicion on anyone who was close enough to be implicated by proximity.

Chance exhaled slowly, letting out a long trail of smoke. He stood before Michaels and Strickler as if delivering a confession.

"It was a bad period in my life," he began. His voice was soft, not trembling, merely threatening to devolve to that. He grabbed the glass of scotch he had brought with him and took a deep swallow. "Things weren't going well, and my writing? Well, the movie industry is a tough enough business to get into when you're young and the opportunity door closes significantly every decade you get older."

"Didn't your father have some money?" Michaels asked.

"He did. But when I refused to follow my brothers into the family business, he cut all ties with me. It didn't matter to me at the time. I was going to make it on my own. But things turned worse."

He gulped another swallow of scotch.

"After more near-misses than I could count, even getting waiter or bartender jobs was difficult. How can you compete against a younger group of better-looking people looking to score it big in Tinsel Town? I was soon living out of my car. Two months later, I sold the car and lived on the streets."

"Jesus, Ethan," Michaels said. This story of hard luck didn't seem like it was going to get better.

"I went to Farnsworth to see if he could help. Just a bit, you know? Just so I didn't have to do things that people do when they need the money bad enough. You know what that son-of-a-bitch did?"

"What did he do, Ethan?" Strickler asked.

"He brought in a kid. Couldn't have been more than eighteen if he was a day. A real waif of a kid. Thin and frail. He said he'd give me double what I asked for if I'd suck the teen's dick. He said it just like that. Said it'd give me character..."

Chance drank more, wiping his mouth where some of the brown liquid ran down one corner and taking a hit off the cigarette. It was a horrible revelation, a confession unlike anything either Michaels or Strickler had heard before. There was some suspicion of Chance's sexual proclivities, but nothing had ever been substantiated. Michaels shifted uncomfortably. He had to ask the question.

"Well? Did you?" he asked his friend.

Chance turned to Michaels. The threat of oncoming tears watered his eyes.

"Fuck you, Bernie," he said. "The only face I have to look at in the mirror is my own. I never hurt anyone that mattered to me. But you have, haven't you? You hurt the one person you should never hurt..."

"Shut up!" Michaels said angrily. He threw his cigarette away. "You don't know what you're talking about. You weren't there."

"I wasn't, you're right," Chance said. "But Farnsworth knew..."

The truth brought Michaels back to the present. He tried to light another cigarette, but his hand trembled too much. Whether that was the result of anger or shame was a matter of interpretation.

"It was a good investment on paper," he said. "I'd done the research."

"But it wasn't," Strickler said. There wasn't judgment in the tone, just the admission of one who had travelled down a similar path with similar results.

"Cyber security startups were popping up like hot cakes. They were all created for the same reason – to sell it to a bigger fish. Most were on the market two years before a big payday for everyone on the ground level. I wanted in on that ground level. It took initial capital, but nothing too big. People were really turning their lives around, regular rags-to-riches."

He inhaled deeply and watched the smoke blow out of his nose. It billowed in the space in front of him, a thick smog of guilt.

"You really think I would have taken my daughter's college fund if I didn't think it was going to succeed? You really think I'd do that to my own flesh and blood?"

He waited for his friends to answer "no" to those questions. But they didn't. They knew their friend's history, and while everyone had matured since their college days, it was apparent that any growth was not that significant. Michaels furiously eyed his friends.

"Assholes...What do you want me to say? What I did was wrong, plain and simple. My daughter suffered for it. My marriage still suffers from it. I – I still suffer from it..."

"And the affairs?" Strickler asked.

Michaels scowled.

"Fuck you, Ted," Michaels said.

His voice cracked at the end. He grabbed Chance's glass of scotch and finished the rest of it in one swallow. Chance didn't try to stop him or say anything about his sobriety. He turned to Strickler who stood on the sideline, perhaps trying to avoid his own confessional.

"Doctor?" Chance addressed the tall man. "You have anything you want to get off your chest?"

Strickler made a dismissive sound.

"If you think I'm going to join this little pity party, you have another thing coming."

"Oh, come on, Teddy. A little catharsis is good for you. Just look at us. We're beaming." Michaels said. "Jump into the nightmare with the rest of us. The water is still warm."

"Kiss my ass, Bernie," Strickler said.

"Make it bare."

The two men got into each other's face. Assuming his traditional role as the group peacemaker, Chance separated the two potential combatants.

"Are we really going to throw punches? At our age? Come on, guys. So, we all had to ask for Farnsworth help. Big deal. Same in college, same in our real lives." Chance turned to Strickler. "You don't have to hide anything from us, Ted. We're your friends."

Strickler snorted.

"Yeah, you're my friends, alright. I haven't seen any of you in nearly forty years. Forty years. What kind of friends are that?"

Chance put a consoling hand on Strickler's shoulder. It seemed to be enough. Strickler opened up.

"When you're a doctor, there's an inordinate amount of pressure...."

"Cut the shit, Ted. We all have pressure."

"Let him speak, Bernie," Chance chastised Michaels. "Go on, Ted."

"Sarah and I – we weren't connecting anymore. We were living in the same house, but we weren't really together, if you know what I mean. We were like ghosts passing by each other, exchanging sparse words only when things needed to be clarified. Anyway, I focused on my practice. You know the story, more time at the office, less time at home. I was making investments, some not so good."

Michaels smiled. Chance looked at him and shook his head. Now was not the time.

"I borrowed money from our joint account," Strickler continued, "fully expecting to pay it back when things turned around. They didn't. And that led to pulling more hours. A never-ending cycle. The hours add up, especially when you're not twenty anymore, and when I managed to find a bed for a nap, my mind raced thinking about all the things I still needed to do. The drugs helped me rest, and when Sarah and I had a huge blowout, Fentanyl was there to take the edge off. And then there was that one opportunity to good to pass up. My wife was adamantly against it. She wouldn't lend me the money. Can you imagine that? Your wife – your partner in life – unwilling to help, and after all the things that I gave her? So, I forged her signature and I got the money. End of story."

He paused to compose himself. This might be his confession, but he would be damned if he showed any vulnerability. Not before these men. Not before Michaels.

"Not quite the end," Michaels said. "What Farnsworth said about malpractice – is that true?"

Strickler's met Michaels' look. He refused to look away.

"Yes."

"Because of your extracurricular activities," Michaels prodded.

"It was a mistake. I can weather the storm. I have to. I don't have anything else."

It was a sentiment that all three men shared. They didn't have anything else. It was a condition they were all familiar with. They were the same in college. Farnsworth recognized that each one of these men was an island unto himself. And in knowing that, Farnsworth saw the potential of cobbling a patchwork friendship with these men. They were the type that desperately wanted the company of others but lacked a quality that others typically sought out. Farnsworth used this neglect to his advantage, bringing them in close. He provided them refuge from other cliques and groups, and in doing so, they empowered him to play his games with them. They had to acquiesce to his wishes; the alternative was something that none of them could handle on their own. And this was the common denominator that escaped the men's attention but was something that Farnsworth knew instinctively. They had no one else and would never have anyone else.

"So," Michaels said after the men had a chance to compose themselves from their admittance of their failures. "Does anyone want to address the elephant in the room?"

"What's that?" Chance asked.

"Come on, Ethan. We're all thinking it," Michaels said. "What the lawyer said. About Farnsworth being murdered."

"Oh, that," Chance said. "I didn't take him seriously. How would he know something like that?"

"He wouldn't," Strickler said. "Unless he did it."

"Maybe," Michaels said.

"You can't really believe that, Bernie," Chance said. "He just arrived here. How would he know? It's probably just a smokescreen."

"Yeah," Michaels mused. "But it makes you think. I mean, why? For what purpose?"

"I don't know. Part of the game maybe," Chance said.

"It's a stretch," Strickler finally spoke up.

"But what if it's not?" Chance pressed on.

"Then that would mean one of us killed him," Michaels said. "We may not be the best friends in the world, but we aren't killers."

"You stated that you had thought about killing him," Strickler countered.

"It was just an expression. Besides, you'd be lying if you didn't think about it at least fifty times."

"What about Zeke?" Chance offered, proud of himself for thinking outside the box. "It could have been Zeke. I mean, what do we really know about him anyway?"

"Shut it, you two. Farnsworth killed himself, okay? He wasn't well. He wasn't well at all."

Chance and Michaels turned to Strickler.

"How do you know that? Did he tell you something?" Michaels asked.

"He didn't have to. The medications he was on? They address fast moving cancer. They're what we call in the profession as 'Hail Marys'. Real long shots."

"What are you saying? He was dying?" Chance asked. The enormity of this bit of information was difficult to get his mind around.

"That's my professional opinion, from just reviewing the drugs," Strickler said.

"But why would the lawyer say he was murdered?" Michaels asked.

"To confuse us. It adds to the game, doesn't it? It's a magician's sleight of hand, a red herring to keep us guessing."

Strickler relished being the center of attention. It was a position he was most comfortable in when surrounded by inferiors.

"And to keep us looking over our shoulders," Chance said. "Intimating that one of us did it makes us distrust one another."

"You mean more than we already do?" Michaels said.

Strickler ignored Michaels and turned to Chance.

"Maybe…but for what purpose?" Strickler asked.

"Are you kidding? There are roughly eight billion of them," Chance said. "So, we wouldn't conspire to divide the money after it's all over."

"We can't," Michaels said. "You heard what the lawyer said."

Strickler let out a laugh. It was more of bark, but it got the other two men's attentions.

"Classic, Farnsworth," he said. "Pit the right hand against the left. Then sit back and watch as they battle it out."

"There's only one problem there," Michaels said. "Farnsworth's dead."

"We saw exactly what Farnsworth wanted us to see," Strickler said. "Think about it. It wouldn't have been the first time we played one of his 'games' to find him at the finish line handing out towels to wipe the egg off our faces."

"He may be dead," Michaels said. "But he's still waiting to see who makes it across the finish line."

*****

Later in the day, Strickler put his coffee cup in the sink. He looked out the window and saw Michaels out back.

"What are you up to, Bernie?" he asked himself. He was going to spy on him from the living room when a better idea crossed his mind. Strickler walked by the dining room, pausing when he saw Chance looking over the clues from the previous two nights.

What are you doing, Ethan?"

"I'm taking these into the game room. I don't have much of an appetite when I see them here."

Strickler said nothing and went upstairs. He walked to Michaels room and checked the door. It was locked. Strickler then went to his room and cut through their joint bathroom to enter Michaels' room from the back end.

Just like Bernie the Burnout, he thought. Locking the front door but always leaving the back door wide open.

Strickler frowned when he saw the state of the room. They hadn't been there more than a couple of days and Michaels had made himself at home. The room was a mess; the bed was in a disheveled state and his clothes and personal effects had been strewn all over floor, as if his suitcase had exploded rather than meticulously unpacked.

He checked the closet, patting down the pockets of the shirts and jacket hanging there. He checked the night table drawers, searching for something, anything that might look out of place. That might make Michaels look…guilty.

He checked the bureau drawer by drawer. The bottom one provided the very thing he was looking for – a flask.

"It's hard to fall off the wagon, Bernie," Strickler said smiling at the find. "When you never planted your ass on it in the first place." He tucked it back under the underwear where he had found it. It wasn't the serendipitous find of the booze that sent a chill up Strickler's spine. Further rummaging provided him something he didn't expect.

A revolver.

Strickler's face grew concerned. Guns were not something with which he associated with Michaels.

Strickler's mind raced.

Why do you have a gun, Bernie? Why would you feel the need to bring a gun to a weekend reunion?

He thought of Farnsworth and what the lawyer had said about murder. The only problem with that scenario was that Farnsworth hadn't been shot.

Which made the question even more prominent – why did you bring a gun?

The question perched on Strickler's mind like a black raven, waiting for its turn to eat from the pile of roadkill.

*****

Chance arranged the clues in the game room as they had been in the dining room. The textbook and the mannequin of the girl. He flipped through the biology book. It seemed standard college fare, albeit outdated. It had been used; passages had been underlined in red pen, and notes were neatly scribbled in some of the page margins. The penmanship had the unmistakable flourish and rounded characters of a woman's hand. None of the underlining or notes seemed to provide any more insight about the game, or the victim in this case. Just a big biology textbook with out of date information.

The mannequin, on the other hand, gave him the willies.

It was grotesque in its authenticity, if that made any sense. The face was remarkably real. The mouth reminded him so much of Munch's impressionistic "The Scream."

Something about what Strickler had said still resonated with him.

We saw exactly what Farnsworth wanted us to see.

Chance furrowed his brows in thought. Everything was done with a specific intent in mind. Things were placed a certain way. Seemingly benign objects were not benign at all and held the most important value, even if it wasn't readily discerned.

What did you want us to see, Farnsworth? What was it you thought we would see…?

*****

Michaels walked around the backyard. Near the barn was a wood pile. Next to that was a stump for chopping logs and un-chopped logs in a pile beside it.

Michaels looked around for their quiet host.

Where is Zeke?

For a big man, he moved quietly. There were no old age grunts or tired joints. He still chopped wood. He still drove. He ran a working farm, at least before his circle intersected with Farnsworth. At his age, it seemed, nothing slowed him down.

Zeke was closer than Michaels knew. The old man stood by the side of the house, the large axe in his hand. It was a staple tool for the area. There wasn't a ten-year-old boy that didn't know how to use an axe.

The city folk didn't know how to use an axe. He'd bet his last cent on that. They couldn't split a cord of wood if their lives depended on it.

Zeke smiled. That was funny. He imagined seeing these clowns frantically trying to chop wood. That Michaels might have a chance. He seemed more-blue collar than the doctor and the effeminate Chance. It was something in the way he carried himself, like he knew what it felt like to carry the weight of the world on his shoulders. Strickler just came off like a snob. He could snap Strickler in his hands like a dried-out twig. And Chance? Well, he had a pretty good idea the type of wood Chance knew how to handle.

Zeke held out the axe in his hand, eyeing the blade against Michaels' head. One downstroke and that head would split like an over-ripe melon. A side-swipe would bury the blade of the axe in Strickler's chest. And a back-swing would fall Chance like a sapling. The entire crew could be wiped out in a matter of seconds.

Zeke laughed much louder than he had expected because Michaels turned around and saw him with the axe outstretched in his hands. The two men made eye contact, trying to read the expression in each other's face.

"How goes it?" Michaels called out to him.

Zeke lowered the axe.

"It goes as it should," Zeke said. "There's always something to be done."

"I guess so," Michaels said. "How are you doing with all of this?"

"How do you mean?"

"It's kind of crazy, isn't it? Seems just too impossible."

Zeke paused. He didn't understand why things seemed so darn-confusing for these supposedly college-educated grown men. If college was all about hand-holding, he wondered why people wanted to go there in the first place.

"Nothing impossible about it," Zeke blustered.

"What do you mean?"

"God's work," Zeke shrugged as if the answer was that simple.

"You think God wanted Farnsworth dead?"

"Each time the Almighty pulls a thread, it's not our place to know if he's taking something apart or weaving something together. Only that we know He is doing His will."

The conviction in Zeke's voice made Michaels quiver.

*****

Chance locked his bedroom door behind him and bee-lined to the bathroom. His was the only room without a bathroom, but he didn't mind walking the short distance to the one at the end of hall. He decided to treat himself to a long hot bath. In the tub, he ran over the events of the day again in his mind. By the time he went through all the details, he felt the dull throb of a headache increasingly pound at his temples.

Michaels took his drink on the porch. Yes, it was the heat of the moment, but for a man fighting for his daily sobriety, he took down a half-glass of scotch like it was nothing. Alcohol made Bernie do some crazy things in college. Once he surpassed a certain amount, he turned into a different person altogether. He was more careless. He took chances. He'd do anything on a dare.

Chance washed his face with a handcloth as he worked through the situation. Sure, it was only a couple of drinks. No big deal. But what if he was drinking more? What if he was drinking when no one saw him, when he could indulge himself without fear of scrutiny.

Chance shivered. His costume depicted a hedonist, someone prone to satisfying his urges.

Alcoholics don't take just one drink.

He had a specific look on the porch when they were sharing their secrets and discussing Farnsworth's death. It was one he was intimately familiar with because he knew he wore the same expression.

Desperation.

Chance climbed out of the tub and grabbed a towel. He methodically dried himself off and walked he short distance to his bedroom. He closed and locked the door behind them, then went straight over to the top drawer of his bureau.

He drew his hand back as if he almost touched a black widow.

On top of his shirt was a magazine. A dirty magazine, to be exact. Chance didn't need to look further to know what this magazine was.

It was a gay bondage magazine. His was in the last layout complete with dog collars, a gag ball, and an assortment of dildoes. It wasn't his finest moment, but he had needed the money. He had been in Los Angeles two years when it all bottomed out. This kept him afloat. Barely.

Chance picked up the magazine and threw it in the garbage. How did it get here, he wondered?

Two names sprang to the forefront. Michaels and Strickler.

He had been certain that no one knew about his foray into gay porn. And even if they did, how would they have gotten their hands on the magazine? There wasn't a wide distribution for content like this. No, no one could have known about this. Not even Farnsworth. There were some distances even Farnsworth's reach couldn't bridge.

And still, the magazine was there, a proverbial slap to his face.

How did this magazine show up in his room?

*****

In the game room, Chance sat at the chess table moving a pawn aimless around on the board. Michaels walked in and headed for the bar. He had already poured himself some bourbon when he saw his friend at the table in the corner.

"You're drinking again," Chance said. It was a comment, not a judgment, and he hoped that Michaels would accept it as so.

"In light of things Ethan, it just seemed like a pretty good idea. That okay with you?"

"I was just making an observation."

"An observation with just a hint of judgment."

"I wasn't judging," Chance said, but then stopped himself. There was no arguing with a drunk.

"Makes you think, doesn't it? I mean, if alcohol is supposed to be a depressant, how come so many fights start because of it?"

"It effects people differently."

"Sure, that makes sense." A pause. "How does it affect you?"

"What do you mean?"

"You were drinking the other night," Chance said. "I could smell it on your breath."

"I had a drink. A drink isn't the same as drinking or being drunk for that matter. I think that even Strickler would attest to that."

"Yeah, but you said you had quit. You made a big deal of making that clear when we got here. Why did you feel you had to lie about something like that?"

"I wish you'd stop dancing around whatever it is you want to say and just get to the point already. Christ, I thought I left my wife at home," Michaels said.

"I'm not that pretty," Chance said, trying to diffuse the increasingly tense situation with a joke.

"Oh, I don't know about that, Ethan," Michaels said. "I'm sure someone is sweet on you."

Chance's eyes narrowed as he wondered the intent behind the remark. Had the Burnout put the magazine in his room? Chance tried to quickly change the subject.

"It's a hell of a game, isn't it?" Chance asked. "Think we'll really figure it out?"

"Someone better," Michaels said. "That's a lot of money to leave on the table."

Chance turned to the game clues he had arranged in the room.

"The pieces are just so different," Chance continued. "They're supposed to fit but don't seem to have any natural harmony. They each have their own mystery, their own secret. Just like people, don't you think?"

"I don't know. Maybe."

"You know what they say about chess? It's the perfect metaphor for life. Competing to get ahead, strategizing for a better advantage, taking chances, sometimes coming out ahead, sometimes losing. How to problem solve in an uncertain environment. Life – it's just one big game, Bernie. Farnsworth recognized it straight off. That's why he excelled at it while the rest of us stood around and gawked."

"Farnsworth wasn't a saint, Ethan. He was the most cut-throat individual I ever met. There were no second-place finish for him, and he couldn't stand anyone that finished in that slot."

Chance smiled wryly.

"Even in death he finished first."

"And trust me. That is one race you don't want to win."

*****

Strickler's hard-planed face gradually softened. His lids grew immediately heavy, and he released a long sigh.

The drug took its familiar hold and his body quickly surrendered to its embrace.

It had been quite a day. Farnsworth was dead in a probable suicide. A strange attorney popped out of nowhere telling them his estate was up for grabs. And Michaels and Chance were typically clueless, rudderless without the maniacal Captain Ahab telling them where to go and what to do. He should have shot up earlier.

The clock on the wall read three o'clock. He had plenty of time before the evening's gaming events.

Why had he waited so long for this fix?

*****

At ten to eight, Quinlan sat patiently in the game room. From his briefcase he removed a large manila envelope, the contents of which would provide the clue to be used for the evening's game.

He looked at the two discovered clues that Chance had relocated to the game room. On the surface, they seemed so mundane, he wondered if these dull men had the mental capacity to draw any conclusions, even if they were just hypothetical. He had to hand it to Farnsworth; the genius of the game lied in its simplicity, relying on high stakes and players committed and obedient to the rules to dictate the flow. After that, the players' reactions to the clues would drive the narrative to its conclusion.

A murder mystery indeed.

"Zeke," Quinlan called out loudly. "Summon the players. It's time to restart the game."

Chapter 10

Strickler was the last to arrive. He was a little "off", unkempt by his standards and rubbing his eyes as if he just woke up from a deeper sleep than he had intended on having. His obvious state alerted both Michaels and Chance that something was not necessarily right with their friend.

"Thank you for joining us, Doctor," Quinlan said, not trying to mask his perturbed tone.

"Apologies," Strickler said. "My body needed more rest than I had anticipated."

Michaels noticed a small red stain on Strickler's shirt sleeve. It looked as if an uncapped red marker had daubed the white cotton. Only it wasn't ink; it was blood.

"You alright, Ted?" he said, pointing to the stain. It was a little red blot at the inside of the elbow. Strickler threw on his jacket.

"Picked a scab," he said, brushing by the comment as he helped himself to a carafe of coffee on the table.

"Gentlemen," Quinlan continued, pointing at the manila envelope. "This is the first of the last two clues."

"Do we really need the ceremony? Can't you just give us both clues now?" Michaels asked.

"That does not follow the dictates of Mr. Farnsworth's instructions."

Michaels pressed on.

"I'm just saying that the clues so far have been pretty ridiculous. A book and a mannequin. They don't mean anything. Why do we have to run around this damn town if we are going to see the clues the next day anyway?"

Quinlan smirked, and walked around the coffee table to face Michaels. The men locked eyes for a moment before Michaels turned away.

"Mr. Farnsworth anticipated that there would be misgivings. Let me assure you that prior to his passing he had complete confidence that at least one of you would solve this mystery. Something about pride in the academic foundation provided by our institution of higher learning."

"Which mystery?" said Chance sardonically. "Solving the game or his death?"

Quinlan released the slightest of smiles. He grabbed the envelope and held it out to the men, waiting for one of them to take it.

"And to answer your question, Mr. Michaels. You have to run around this 'damn town' as you aptly put it because that is what Mr. Farnsworth wanted. And if you want a chance at his fortune, then you will do exactly as is instructed."

Strickler grabbed the envelope from his hand and opened it. A green plaid patterned Catholic school girl's uniform spilled out onto the table.

"What the hell's that?" Michaels asked.

"I believe that is something for you to figure out. Oh, and another thing. I must inform you that the rules have changed slightly."

"Of course," Strickler said. "What now?"

Quinlan produced a letter from inside his suit jacket pocket.

"As dictated by Mr. Farnsworth's instructions, if you care to take a look."

Strickler shook his head. He didn't need to see the new dictates. He needed to buy time to get his head clear. His second cup of coffee was beginning to take hold, slowly shaking the haze free.

"What are the new rules?" Michaels asked.

"Instead of competing individually, you will be working collaboratively as a team. No more indiscriminate drop-offs in random parts of this quaint town. You will go out collectively and find the object in question collectively. All three initials must be present at the object's designated marker."

"That doesn't make sense. How can one of us win if we have to work together?"

"Just because you find the clues doesn't mean that you know how to put them together the correct way, as evidenced by Mr. Michaels' earlier outburst."

"Seems like we heard that before," Strickler mused.

"You don't honestly think you were just going to find clues and that was going to be it? Four objects found and the game ends. No, Mr.

Farnsworth was not going to spoon-feed you eight billion dollars. Doctor, you disappoint me."

"Was this always the plan?" Chance asked. "I mean, if Farnsworth hadn't…you know…were we always supposed to work as a team or is this your addition?"

"I only know what my directions are," said Quinlan noncommittedly.

"Sure it was," Michaels said. "Think about it, Ethan. He pulls us together after all these years knowing full well that none of us had seen each other, that we all had financial problems, that we were all were very desperate. And then he invites us here, and which one of us wasn't going to jump at the opportunity of maybe getting him alone and asking just one more time for help. And what's he go and do? He does us one better – one million dollars payout to whoever wins his game. One million! I'm sure he loved the expressions on our faces when he told us that. But that isn't enough for Farnsworth. And then the twist of all twists – he kills himself. I mean, honestly, which one of us saw that coming? And so here we are now, the prize escalated once more, and we are now forced to finish the game together where we are at our most competitive, and you're telling me you don't see it?"

"No," Chance said with a perplexed expression. "I don't."

"He wants us to turn on each other," Michaels said.

Chance shook his head. It was hard to believe. Too far-fetched even for someone like Farnsworth to plan that far in advance.

"What are you talking about, Bernie? That's crazy..." he said.

"Is it? What makes you think so? How is this any crazier than anything else he ever put us through?"

Chance tripped over his words. The more he thought, the more he couldn't think of a reasonable explanation of why Farnsworth wouldn't do this. When he understood that truth, he shut his mouth. Michaels turned to Strickler.

"Doctor?"

Strickler didn't say a word. He knew that Michaels was probably right; he just didn't feel the need to publicly tell Michaels that to his face. He instead turned to Quinlan. The lawyer smiled bashfully, as if caught in a white lie.

"That's a bit melodramatic," Quinlan said. "I think it's better to frame this little competition as a battle of wills. A battle of intelligence. Of psyche. Of resolve. And to the victor goes unlimited spoils. I don't have to remind you how much money is at stake."

He was right and they knew it. All three turned to look at the plaid-green school uniform on the table. It had dirt and dried mud on it. Two noticeable tears frayed the hem of the skirt. The object was frightful in what it intimated rather than what it was. It made their minds wander, to fill in the empty spaces.

"Well, gentlemen? Shall we proceed?" Quinlan said, tapping the face of his large Rolex watch. "Time is ticking."

*****

In the back of the van, Strickler held the schoolgirl uniform in his hands. There wasn't much discussion between them. Each man was in a contemplative mood, content to stay within the confines and security of his own thoughts. Collaboration would have to be carefully calculated and implemented with a deft hand; they all had to balance sharing some without sharing too much. Besides, silence seemed appropriate and respectful for this article of clothing. It might be just a piece of cloth, but it was a girl's, and in that knowledge, it just seemed better to avoid the use of any impolite language or sentiment.

Michaels dug into his pocket and removed the silver flask. He took a drink and caught Strickler's gaze. He held the flask out to the doctor, who shook his head and let out an exasperated sigh.

"What can I say? The cat's out of the bag. I'm still drinking," Michaels said. "It's my third in case you were keeping count."

Chance quickly interjected before the men got into another argument.

"No one's keeping count. But maybe you should put a pause on that," he said. "We have to solve the puzzle, and I think it's going to take all of our wits to figure this thing out."

"I don't know, Ethan," Michaels said. "Alcohol unstraps the mind's limitations."

"No," Strickler said. "It just makes you think you are more creative."

"Not entirely true, Doctor," Michaels countered. "Wasn't it Hemingway that said, 'write when drunk, edit when sober'?"

"Didn't Hemingway eat the end of a shotgun? You know what? You're right, Bern'. Have another drink," Strickler said. "One less person in my way to the prize."

The remark hit its mark. Michaels capped the flask and put it back in his pocket.

"It was a drink. Not a fifth. Not a bottle. Just a drink."

Strickler tugged at the collar of his shirt. It was obviously rubbing his neck the wrong way, kind of like Michaels only less offensive.

"Polyester," Strickler hissed. "I hate this shirt."

"So, change it," Michaels said.

"To what? Did you bring a spare change of clothes?"

Chance looked at Michaels and Strickler. All of them were still in the costumes they were directed to bring. It was evident that the men brought only those items that reflected the character they portrayed.

"Huh," Chance said. Their clothes struck him as funny. He looked at his outfit, and the outfits of the others.

"What is it, Ethan?" Michaels asked.

"Our clothes."

"What about them?"

"Doesn't it seem almost desperately random that we had to dress like this? I mean, unless I'm wrong, this has nothing to do with solving the mystery, right?"

"The suit said it was to reveal our dirty laundry to one another. A Farnsworth dig, so to speak."

"Yeah, I know," Chance said. "But what if it wasn't? What if the clothes themselves are clues to the puzzle?"

An interesting hypothesis. Michaels sat up straight.

"What do you mean?"

"Hear me out. None of us brought a change, which meant we had to stay in character. And our characters were extreme representations of our secrets." He took the uniform from Strickler's hands. "What's this representation?"

"A girl scout," Strickler said.

"A schoolgirl's uniform," Michaels offered.

"A *Catholic* schoolgirl's uniform," Chance corrected. "The mannequin was a girl. This is a girl's school uniform."

Michaels followed.

"A biology textbook," Michaels said.

"I think we're getting somewhere," Chance said. He sat back in his seat, thumbing at his satin robe. "You know, I never shared turning tricks with anyone, and I certainly wouldn't have let Farnsworth know so he could spend the rest of my life picking at that scab. We kept these close to the vest, so to speak, and yet he found out. How?"

The men didn't have an answer. In driver's seat, Zeke mumbled something that caught the attention of the men in back.

"What's that?" Strickler asked.

Zeke adjusted the rearview mirror so the men in back could see his eyes.

"I said, it's like the old saying goes: the more you try to conceal something, the harder it wants to come out."

"Are you saying that we wanted to expose our own secrets?"

"I didn't say that," Zeke said. "You just did."

*****

An hour-and-a-half had passed, and the contestants were no further along than they were when Zeke dropped them off in front of the bar and grill. The lights were on and music could be heard from the jukebox inside. They didn't bother sticking their heads in the door and peeking. Avoiding distraction was of paramount importance.

Instead, the men wandered around, jumping on Chance's hunch. They went to both the elementary and middle schools without luck. They tried a small clothing store next (they tried the department store, but the door was locked) but was shut down there as well. Chance brought up trying the East Bumfuck church, but that too was a dead end. What was a fruitful list of possibilities all turned to verifiable mush. Three strikes and they were literally down-and-out.

"Ninety minutes left," Chance said, looking at the large clock at the corner of the part at the center of town.

"Anybody have any other ideas?" Strickler said.

Chance and Michaels let their joint silence answer the doctor's question.

"We checked every door, every window," Chance asked hopefully. "Is there any chance that there's been a mistake?

Michaels shook his head as he lit a cigarette.

"No," he said. "Farnsworth was always fair, even in his cruelty. He wouldn't have the prize behind a locked door. That wouldn't be sporting."

Strickler grit his teeth. Michaels' smug tone was the last straw in a series of straws, any of which could have snapped the camel's back.

"Two days of you, Bernie, and I don't think I can stand another word out of your fucking mouth."

The remark had no visible effect on Michaels, who only smirked at the doctor.

"If you think I'm flip now, Teddy, wait 'til you see me when I move onto Tequila."

"I saw you drunk three straight years in college, Bernie," Strickler seethed. "Cleaned up a few of your messes too. See you on Tequila? Hell, I picked you up from it."

Michaels face darkened.

"Listen to me you sanctimonious prick...." Michaels voice rose as he got into Strickler's face.

Forever the peacemaker, Chance inserted himself in between the two men before they embarrassed themselves.

"Hold it! Hold it a second, will you? Fighting each other isn't going to accomplish anything."

"I beg to differ," Strickler said. "People can't speak too well with broken jaws."

"And who's going to give me one, Ted? You? When's the last time you punched anyone that could punch back?"

"Give me the chance, and you'll see."

"I'm right here, asshole."

"Why don't we just split it!" Chance yelled. It wasn't often that the most reserved of the three friends felt compelled to do things out of character. Screaming wasn't part of his usual repertoire, so when he did give himself that luxury, it usually succeeded in garnering the attention of the others.

"The money," he continued. "Why don't we just divvy it up?"

"What are you talking about?" Strickler asked.

"Hear me out," Chance said. "For whatever reason, Farnsworth wanted us to fight it out like we're doing now. That fits into his plan. So, let's change it up. We work together, pick someone to win, and then split up the company, or at least get a hefty payout from the person that owns it. Not immediately. We want to make sure that the probationary period passes. And when it does, money gets distributed."

The plan sounded good. Still. What the attorney said lingered on the minds of Michaels and Strickler.

"You heard the attorney; it doesn't work that way."

"He said it *doesn't*. Who says it *can't*? We can make it happen if we want to make it happen."

Strickler asked the question that was on the tips of all their tongues.

"Who gets to win?"

"What does it matter?" Chance asked. "I can live with a third of eight billion. Hell, I can live with half of a third."

"It damn well matters, Ethan. How can the other two be assured that whoever wins won't just skip with the rights to the inheritance? It's not like we can sign a legal document and sue."

"Jesus, Ted," Chance said, legitimately hurt. "We know each other. We're friends."

"You keep saying that, but none of us has seen the other in years. In *years*. Hell, Ethan. We didn't even know enough about each other to know that Farnsworth was playing us for suckers."

Chance could not counter that truth. He looked away, watching the fragile construct of his plan dissipate in the air, never to be retrieved again.

"The shame," he said to whoever was listening. "I hate it. I hate myself."

"Don't," Michaels said. "Farnsworth knew our secrets because we went to him for things like common street panhandlers. In school...now... How could he not want us to see us twist at the end of his stick? You talk about friends, Ethan. None of us went to each other for help. We went to him. And in doing so we knowingly gave him power. What does that say about us?"

Michaels stepped to the side and took a deep drag off his cigarette. Strickler turned to Chance.

"I think what Bernie means is that money never makes friendships, but it certainly is instrumental in ending them."

Chance didn't hide the tears running down his cheeks. He didn't feel the need to hide anything anymore.

"My God," he said. "We were Farnsworth's friends."

"Yeah," Strickler said. "And look where that got him."

Maybe it was the way in which he said, or the tone with which he said it with, but Chance shot Strickler a questioning look.

*****

The men sat next to each other on the street curb. Strickler looked at the uniform in his hands and tossed it to the ground.

"It's useless," he said. "I give up."

"So much for the old college try," Michaels said.

"Fuck you, Bern'."

"Ted, I've been fucked since we graduated. I've become accustomed to that feeling."

Chance said nothing. He looked at the uniform on the ground. It looked lost and out of place in this environment. And yet it still permeated a sense of power. It didn't have a voice but that didn't mean it couldn't speak. It did. It spoke volumes. But what struck Chance was how dirty it was, an interesting juxtaposition considering the image Catholicism projected combined with the perception of Catholic girls being chaste, pure, and clean.

"What is this object?" he said aloud suddenly, picking up the uniform.

"What's he babbling about?" Strickler asked Michaels. Michaels shrugged and shook his head.

"Follow me here," Chance continued. "We checked the schools. None of them were Catholic. So, the uniform didn't come from there. It didn't come from the children's clothes store either, or the department store, or any other store for that matter."

"What's your point?" Strickler said.

Chance's face brightened.

"Maybe it has nothing to do with something new, per se, but something old."

"Go on, Ethan," Michaels said.

"Okay, let's take this at face value. It's a Catholic girl's school uniform. It's torn. It's filthy."

"So?"

"So...Maybe it has to be...clean?"

"Clean?"

Chance nodded his head.

"Clean."

The men exchanged hopeful looks. At least it was another lead to follow.

*****

Outside the East Bumfuck laundromat, the men found the front door locked, as well as the backdoor typically used by the maintenance staff. There were no windows that could be opened that would provide an alternative access inside the facility. They had run into another dead end.

"Brilliant deduction, Sherlock," Strickler quipped after kicking the front door in frustration. He checked his watch. "Eighteen minutes until the fat lady sings."

Chance shook his head. He thought that he had it.

"I was so sure…"

Michaels slapped his friend on the back in support.

"Let's go take our medicine," Strickler said. "But I swear if that fucking lawyer makes one snide remark, I'm going to lose it."

Michaels took the uniform from Chance and felt it in his hands, prepared to toss it into the first trash can he saw. The fabric was thick to the touch and hard. It needed more than a good washing, it needed the stringent steam and chemicals of a dry-cleaning press.

"Ow!" he said. He looked inside the uniform's collar where his finger had been pricked by something sharp. He found a small tag stapled to the tab. It was red with a number that was barely legible to the eye.

"What do you make of this?" Michaels asked holding up the tag to his friends.

"I don't know, it looks like a – "

"Dry-cleaning tag," Strickler said. "It's a dry-cleaning tag."

The three men looked across the street where East Bumfuck Dry Cleaning neon-sign flashed quietly and unassumingly in the darkness.

"Fifteen minutes," Michaels said. "Let's go."

The three men ran across the street and stood in front of the door. A sign was proudly displayed in the window:

East Bumfuck Dry Cleaning
What You Want, When You Want
Toughest Stains Clean or Your Money Back
Clothes Pressed Upon Request

"Here goes nothing," Chance said.

His hand tried the handle and the door easily pulled open. The men all shared an excited look, and for a moment, their faces were devoid of any suspicion or cunning and beamed with the expectation of unearthing buried treasure.

Inside, Michaels tried the lights. The switch flicked but no illumination ensued.

"Of course," he mumbled.

Like fireflies in the approaching night, one by one the men turned their penlights on. Three separate beams cut through darkness, illuminating the counter, the completed dry-cleaning hanging on racks, the tailor station, the changing room.

"Let's divide and conquer," Strickler said. He then took of his coat and rolled up his sleeves. "Jesus, it's hot in here."

All three separated and looked around the room. It was hard enough to try to find a needle in a haystack and even more difficult when said haystack was dispersed over a two thousand square foot space. Chance checked a wall where boxes of cobbled shoes waited for patron pick-up and started scanning through the numbers on the sides.

"What's the number on the tag?" he asked.

Michaels checked.

"B-0-2-4-7-8."

Strickler decided to concentrate on the corner of the room that had recent deliveries of clothing items that had been outsourced to another location. He ran a light over the numbers attached to the bags and boxes on the floor.

Michaels inspected the conveyor where most of the finished dry-cleaning hung, draped in clear plastic wrapping. He found the switch but couldn't get it turned on.

"Anyone work one of these gizmos before?"

Chance went over and inspected the machinery.

"This is a multi-plan double deck Shuffle-form system. You have to turn this switch here, and then hit that button."

Chance flicked the switch and pressed the button. The garment conveyor roared into life, giving the men a startle. He looked at Michaels and smiled.

"Two years at the Ritz Cleaners in Santa Monica. 'Fashion Sits at The Ritz.'"

"Jesus, Ethan," Strickler said. "Is there a place you haven't worked?"

Chance made a face at him and touched another button on the switch, causing the turnstile started spinning in overdrive. He made a correction, stopping the turnstile, and adjusted the direction, slower this time.

"I'm a bit rusty," he said. Michaels focused his light on the tags, checking them periodically. Strickler checked his watch.

"Eight minutes left."

"Come on, come on," Michaels urged.

The "B" Section came around next. Stricker joined Michaels in checking the numbers on the tags with the one in the schoolgirl uniform.

"Give me some light here," he said.

Chance shined his light on Strickler. Michaels noticed a fresh set of track marks on his arm. A puzzled look crossed his face. Strickler caught Michaels staring and rolled down his sleeves.

"You going to give me a hand here, or what?"

Michaels dove back in. He found it on the fifth try.

"I have it," he said and removed a black garment bag from the turnstile. He brought it to a table and the men gathered around it.

"It's not going to open itself," Strickler said, taking it on himself to drag the zipper down. He dug into the bag and removed a woman's white blouse. It was freshly cleaned, but the hems of both shoulders were torn, and the front was missing four buttons. The men stared at the shirt; confusion etched on their faces.

"Anybody have an idea of what this is?"

"Besides a lawsuit waiting to happen if these clowns messed up this shirt that badly? No."

Chance just shook his head.

"Well, I know one thing," Strickler said, as the men headed for the front door.

"What's that, Ted?" Chance asked.

"Farnsworth was insane."

*****

The men were ten minutes late for the pickup. Zeke sat in the van with the door open. He spat out a wad of tobacco juice from his mouth as the men approached. Some of the splatter hit Strickler's designer shoes. Zeke was not happy.

"You're late," he said, climbing out from behind the steering wheel and opening the side of the van for the men.

"We're here, aren't we?" Strickler said. He climbed into the van.

Zeke stopped Michaels before he got inside.

"What's the problem with Mr. Manners?" he said, gesturing to Strickler.

"He's a dick, and it's been a long night," Michaels said.

"You fellows find what you were supposed to or what?"

"Ta-daaaa," Chance said. "He held up the blouse for Zeke to see. The old man's eyes got hard, and his face tightened as he clenched his jaw tightly. Then he shook his head and spit again.

"Well how about that."

"Zeke, that hurts. You didn't think we'd find it?"

"That lawyer didn't. Now he owes me twenty bucks. Come on," he said getting behind the wheel of the van.

The ride back to the inn was very quiet. Strickler stared out the window, avoiding any eye contact with the others. Michaels removed his flask and took a drink. The burn was a welcome distraction to the sick feeling in his stomach. He looked at Strickler's arms. The tracks looked fresh in his estimation. Maybe a day or two old, tops. Michaels fought the urge to smile. The good doctor was back on the dope, or better, had never broken its connection. While he took pleasure in that knowledge, it was brief. As he sipped from the flask, his own hypocrisy was not lost.

Chance was the only one still looking at the blouse. It was just a generic blouse. There was nothing fashionable or unique about it, per se. This wasn't the shirt of an ambitious professional climbing the ladder of success, nor was it the attire of one who had already made that ascension. It was something that a young woman would wear at casual gatherings or just puttering around the house. If

Chance was being honest, it was a gesture that fell well below Farnsworth's norm of the extravagant. So, why was it here and what did it have to do with a textbook and a mannequin?

None of these clues made any damn sense. There was nothing that seemed to tie these clues together. And the fact that the clues seemed so desperately random convinced Chance that there was a fine thread tying them all together. A thread that if pulled correctly would unweave this tapestry and reveal everything.

He knew he was close. And he knew that the others were nowhere near putting it all together.

He almost kicked himself for offering to split the company between them all.

It was there in front of him. He just had to look close enough to figure it out.

Chapter 11

Chance followed the men inside the inn but headed immediately upstairs rather than convening in the game room for a post-conference pow-wow. Something nagged at the recesses of his mind that he couldn't quite put his finger on. That blouse had nudged it loose, but it still didn't give all the way. And one thing was for sure – sitting in a room and watching Strickler and Michaels bicker was not going to shake it free.

Chance went to the bathroom and ran the water at the sink. Once it reached a satisfactory lukewarm temperature, he splashed several handfuls of water onto his face. He stared at his reflection, watching drops run from his nose and ears.

He pulled back the skin under and around his eyes. Then he lifted his chin high to try to pull tightly the loose fold that hung just under the ridge.

He sighed heavily. When did he get so old?

*****

Michaels looked at the items in the game room. They conveyed no meaning to him, no specific message that he could take and re-arrange like some visual jumble. Strickler stood reviewing the items with one hand resting under his chin. It made him look like he was assessing a piece of art, standing with objective authority as to the merit of a seemingly careless brushstroke. One thing was evident: the addition of another puzzle piece hadn't made the picture emerge any clearer than before.

"I'm tapped," Michaels said. "The hamsters are spinning those wheels in my head so fast I can smell the smoke. How about a nightcap?" He grabbed a bottle and a glass from the wet bar and poured a stiff shot.

Strickler turned to Michaels. The doctor looked at him emotionlessly as if reading a patient's test result. It was a face that couldn't be read, with no subtle tells to give away the slightest inclination of what he was thinking or feeling. The coldness of the stare gave the normally obnoxious Michaels a shiver.

"You know," Strickler said. "You keep drinking like that and you're going to die a horrible, horrible death."

"Really?" Michaels said, shifting uncomfortably. "Is there a death that isn't horrible?"

"The final stages of liver cirrhosis are a fascinating decline. Have you seen it? No, of course not. How could you? But I have. Such a messy progress. The condemned is prone to easy bleeding or bruising."

"Condemned?" Michaels remarked.

"What would you call a person that repeats the same error until he dies?"

"A connoisseur."

"Joke all you want. It's a steady decline. Especially when jaundice sets firmly in. Yellowing of the skin and eyes is hard to imagine until you see it. All that excess of the pigment bilirubin really perverts the body. And then there's the itching. Think poison ivy but much more robust and in places that you can't scratch. A torture on par with Tantalus in hell itself. You won't want to eat. You can't. The nausea is just too intense. Each time you throw up a little more of you disappears and is flushed down the toilet. Your stomach and legs swell due to fluid buildup. And as you watch your body break down and betray you, your mind follows that path. It's hard to concentrate, to remember. And then it happens - complete shutdown. The final curtain."

The words had been said with such malevolent indifference, that they grabbed Michaels and shook him at the core. When he finally regained his composure, he set his unfinished drink down.

"Fuck you, Ted," he said and walked out of the room toward the stairs.

Strickler smirked. In the never-ending battle of insults that had started more than forty years prior over leftover pizza after a keg party, Strickler had endured his share of losses.

This was not one of them.

Before leaving the game room, Strickler regarded the found items of the Farnsworth ceremonial scavenger hunt. Three objects to solve a case. A book. A mannequin. A blouse.

Who cared?

Strickler snorted and left the room. He waited enough time until he was positive that Michaels was in his room before he started up the stairs.

*****

Michaels stared at the gun. He didn't know how it got there. He hadn't brought it, that's for sure. Hell, he had never even fired a gun before. Well, not a handgun. He had fired .22 caliber rifles at summer camp when he was twelve, but the snub-nosed nickel-plated .38 was in a completely different league. It was a detective's gun, a mobster's gun, a thief's gun. Michaels was none of these things.

Michaels lifted the gun and hefted the weight in his hand. The pearl handle was a nice touch to an already shiny piece. It was a little over a pound he guessed. A popped cylinder revealed that all six chambers had bullets.

Who put it there?

He couldn't see Chance planting the weapon, as a joke or whatever. Guns were not something he associated his friend with. And Strickler wouldn't do it. There wasn't an angle for him to play with that, especially since based on the history of their animosity, Strickler would be the most likely person shot now that Farnsworth had passed on to the Big Nowhere. That only left Zeke, which made less sense considering he had just met the old man a few days ago, and there was no reason whatsoever for him to

219

leave a gun on top of his pajamas in the bureau drawer.

Michaels didn't have a clue. Unfortunately for him, it was a feeling with which he was all too familiar.

*****

Chance retrieved a glass of warm milk from the kitchen with the full intention of going back to his room to try to get some sleep. However, the game room was too much of a distraction, and he found himself sipping from the glass with his eyes fixed on the items on display. It didn't surprise him that Farnsworth had the foresight not to care if the final clues were presented to the men as a group. They all could have been given collectively, negating the need of the men running around town like chickens with their heads cut off, fighting a ticking clock that held no bearing to the progression of the game. But that would have been ultimately boring for Farnsworth's sadistic voyeurism. No, the lawyer had it right. Just because they had the clues in front of them didn't get the men any closer to solving the puzzle. Chance was damn sure the other men were in the same boat as him.

Chance looked around the room, giving his eyes a break from the disturbing items that had commanded so much of their attention. He found the photograph that Zeke took of the men the very first day. In the picture the men were smiling for the camera. Farnsworth's was the biggest of course, a wide shit-eating grin that said, "I know more than you". There had been few smiles since then. How so much had changed so quickly.

Chance studied the photograph. Farnsworth seemed so alive then. And why shouldn't he? He was in his element – his minions summoned to him, ready to be at his beck and call, knowing that they still wanted things from him that only he could provide, and subsequently, refuse them at whim. He hadn't changed at all since college – but to be fair, had any of them really? Michaels was stuck in a never-ending rut and Strickler was as self-destructive as ever. Farnsworth was richer, older, but still the same manipulative prick.

And one more thing. His body had worn down. Chance looked at the photograph and more specifically, at Farnsworth and his cane. He purposefully evaded every question regarding his leg or the reason for his need of a cane. Then there were his sporadic coughing fits. The pain he tried so hard to conceal in front of the men. His inexplicable absences from the group for long periods of time. Any one of these meant nothing on its own, but taken collectively, painted a picture of a man who had passed a line over which he could not go back.

Strickler said Farnsworth was taking serious painkillers.

How did he know that?

He had to have been in Farnsworth's room. Chance had never seen Farnsworth with a pill bottle.

Farnsworth's room. That was a clue in and of itself.

An ambitious idea formulated in Chance's mind. He knew it was ambitious because he was not one prone to bold acts, and this was certainly out of his wheelhouse.

But the one thing he learned from his roommate of three years was that "no one achieved anything that didn't put his balls on the edge of a razor".

Not Farnsworth's most pithy expression, but one whose merits were rooted in historical truth.

Chance removed his shoes and stepped carefully like a cat up the creaky wooden stairs. He purposefully avoided the center spots placing his sock covered feet at the edges of the planks to minimize potential noise.

He strategically crept down the hallway in the same manner, moving almost soundlessly as he passed Michaels' and Strickler's rooms. He didn't want any unexpected guests or questions. There was something he needed to see for himself in Farnsworth's room. Almost giddy, Chance proceeded up the next flight of steps. No one would ever suspect Chance of such bold move as this. He was too wrapped up in self-satisfaction to hear the low creak of a bedroom door opening behind him just for an instant before quietly closing shut.

Chance stood before Farnsworth's bedroom door. Yellow police tape made an "X" at its threshold, barring entry. Chance tested the doorknob. It wasn't locked. He opened the door and stepped through the space between the tape careful not to tear it.

Despite its opulence, the bedroom resembled more of a crypt then a refuge for the master of the house. Chance couldn't help but feel the familiar tingle of fear, though there was nothing that he could put a finger on which he should be afraid. Still, he moved prudently and tentatively in the unfamiliar surroundings. Getting there was one thing; finding what he was searching for – whatever that may be – was a different animal altogether.

His eyes darted about looking for the possible. He rummaged drawers and closets, acknowledging that he was more moving fabric than sifting through the silt to find the shiny gold color at the bottom of the pan. But each opportunity of discovery only yielded the revelation of expensive clothes and accessories.

He found more promise at the night table next to the elevated bed. The top drawer contained a variety of prescription medicine. Bingo. Chance glanced over the names. Nothing seemed out of the ordinary. There were pills for reducing cholesterol, others to combat inflammation, and still others to overcome insomnia issues.

But there was one that he never heard of. He looked at the bottle and tried to pronounce the name.

"Phalomine," he said.

Chance dug into his pocket and removed his smartphone. He got on a web browser and typed in P-h-a-l-o-m-i-n-e and waited for the results. Blue links appeared on the screen, and Chance scrolled down the list. He chose one from a respectable sounding medical site and started to read. One he read that he found another. And then another.

Each site told the same story about the drug. Each site offered the same conclusion.

It was experimental. It was in its initial trial stages. It was unproven.

One thing was clear after the sixth article – Farnsworth was dying. He couldn't pronounce the affliction from which his friend had suffered, but it was a painful deterioration process with a high mortality percentage.

Strickler was right in describing the drug as a "Hail Mary".

Chance looked up from the phone's screen. No wonder Farnsworth had killed himself. Death was bad enough, but the path he was headed down would have made that journey unbearable, bedridden and without dignity. Better to die on your feet, so to speak, then wilt in a bed.

Chance headed toward the door when another thought popped into his head. Farnsworth knew he was dying. Based on what Chance read, he had to know about his condition well before he set up this little reunion. That would explain his desire to sign over his company to the winner, but it seemed an odd way to go about identifying an heir. To serve as guinea pigs that tested the merits of a game was one thing; to pilot that same game with the purpose of willing a Fortune 500 company based on solving a mystery seemed too trite for Farnsworth's normal careful calculation.

This understanding, this admission, could only mean one thing as Chance saw it.

"Attrition" was more than a game.

And then it hit Chance with the force of a thunderbolt. He steadied himself against the doorframe, as his heart thudded against his chest, and perspiration immediately beaded on his upper lip. He closed his eyes to maintain his focus as waves of nausea overwhelmed him and his head spun. He wanted to throw up so badly, but there would be time for that later.

Once the panic attack passed, he grabbed a piece of paper and a marker and hastily wrote a note. Then he exited the room and went downstairs.

Chance looked at the note in his hands as he stood between Michaels' and Strickler's doors.

Meet me outside in ten minutes next to the barn.
I know what's going on.

He folded the paper and looked at the doors in front of him. He had to share his thoughts with one of them, but which? Whom did he trust more?

After what seemed forever, he slid the note under one of the doors, rapping on it twice with his knuckles before he went downstairs.

*****

Outside, Chance's hands shook as he tried to light a cigarette from the pack Michaels had left on the kitchen table. Nervous energy returned and forced him to hold onto the plastic lighter's flame before touching it to the cigarette end. He took two quick puffs, hoping the nicotine would cause that brief hit of a dopamine brain-reward to control his breathing. He washed down the puff with a bottle of bourbon he had taken from the bar.

The barn provided enough privacy to suit the needs at hand. It was dark and far enough removed from the main house so that even if someone was up and looked out their windows, they would not see the rendezvous taking place.

Behind him, the loud snap of a twig captured his attention. He spun around and saw that his invitation had been accepted.

"You scared me half to death," Chance said, taking a deeper drag off his cigarette. He regarded the tobacco stick in his hand. "I tried to quit after college, but no one quits smoking the first few times they try. After the third time, I just stopped trying.

Smoking does a lot to take your mind off things, especially things you don't like to think about. Trust me on that. You know what we used to say in my former profession? 'Habits are like dicks. They should always die hard'."

Chance laughed bitterly. The Figure took a step closer to him. He said something, and Chance nodded as he exhaled. He took another drink from the bottle.

"Something about the way Farnsworth died didn't sit right with me. It kept rattling around my head. The cane. His coughing fits. The way he kept to his room when he wasn't overseeing the game. None of us asked him what was going on, none of us really pressed him on the issue. To be honest, none of us probably cared. We're all older, and if his life took him down a path that made him a bit more broken then the rest of us, well, none of us was losing any sleep over it."

Chance lit a new cigarette off the old one.

"Farnsworth was definitely dying. He had this strange incurable disease. That medication was 'out there', I mean, real crazy stuff. He didn't have much time left I'm guessing. So, it would make sense that he wanted to take his own life, ending things on his terms in a manner of his choosing. But then I got thinking. For a man who liked games, or who liked to see how people reacted from them, suicide seemed too clear cut a resolution for someone of Farnsworth's tastes. He would never allow a game to end so…neatly. Especially if he wasn't going to be there for the end. It would be like cheating somehow. Does that make sense? Which means the only other possible solution like the lawyer said is that one of us killed him."

Again, the Figure responded to Chance who waved him off.

"I'm not saying that's what happened, I'm just pointing out that it is a possible solution. And if you think about it, it's not terribly outlandish. The amount of shit that we ate because of him was more than justification for his life to be ended by anyone who was endlessly persecuted by his hand."

Chance sucked the cigarette down farther.

"But here's the kicker. I can solve the game. I know who the victim is, and I know who killed her. I figured it out. I can win…God, all that money. No more problems. No more worries. No more having to debase myself to certain…acts. It can all go away. Like a dream, it can all be taken by the wind. Everything in the past washed away clean like sins.

Chance's voice trembled. He quickly brushed away tears from his eyes with the back of his hand.

"Funny thing is I don't want the money now. It's not worth it. I don't want to touch a single dime because I figured out the game. That fucking Farnsworth. He got the last laugh alright. Even in death he's laughing his ass off."

Chance drank deeply from the bottle, the alcohol burning his throat and making tears form in his eyes.

"Attrition," he said, fighting through the burn. "You know what that means? 'Forced atonement'."

He lifts the cigarette to his mouth and looks at the scar on his wrist.

"Some people hate scars. They're frightened of them. They're like twisted, vicious grins on the skin. But not me. There's a tremendous amount of importance in a scar. There's always a story that goes with it. A memory. No matter how hard you try to forget something, a scar will always bring you back to a moment. And that's what's truly frightening. Because they remind you of the past and the places you've been, and some of those aren't always pleasant to revisit. Because the person you were then isn't the same one as who you are now. But the past won't ever let you forget. Because the fact is that scars are as ugly as people. And some people are truly hideous. Deep down, they are black."

He held up his arm and rolled down the sleeve.

"Do you remember when we got these?"

No answer from the Figure. Chance looked out into the night. It was peaceful out here, there was no denying that. This was a place where you could lose yourself in the repetition of simple work. Where someone could retreat and never be found or heard from again.

"My God, the woods are beautiful. Listen – crickets, owls, creatures all fidgeting together somewhere out there in the deep lush folds. You can be by yourself out here and never feel quite alone. There's always something that speaks to you from someplace you can't quite see or remember. That much I've learned."

Chance didn't have the opportunity to take a final drag from his smoke. It all happened too quickly. The rope appeared around his throat so fast, so suddenly, there wasn't a second to react. When it pulled tightly, Chance couldn't help but think its snug fit resembled a tie knot pulled too tightly. Lack of oxygen came quickly, and he sank to his knees. There was no urge for fight or flight. Not now. Chance just wanted to stare at the night for as long as he could, hoping that its tranquility would somehow wash over him, and in doing so, provide the respite in death that he couldn't ever achieve in life.

*****

The next day, the search of the house did not yield any significant results. As far as any of them could tell, Chance had not slept in his bed and therefore probably didn't spend the night in his room. All of the effeminate man's clothes were in the drawers or hanging neatly in the closet. Zeke found the gay porn magazine, making a face before tossing it in the garbage. Quinlan frowned at the revelation of Chance's absence. One of the contestants wasn't present, and that gave him cause for concern.

The truck was still parked in the gravel driveway and Zeke insisted that he had the only key, which was typically kept in his vest pocket. The walk to town was only a mile away, and after some goading, Michaels, Strickler, and Zeke made the trip to see if they could find the third contestant, and their friend.

They walked the familiar streets, which looked different in the sunlight. They usually saw the town when shadows ran long, and the silence was ominous. In the daylight, there was pedestrian activity and car traffic moving in both lanes of the two main roads. At night, it looked as if a zombie apocalypse had occurred. Michaels marveled at how the citizens took the East Bumfuck moniker in stride, going on about their daily lives as if they didn't see the change, or at least, didn't acknowledge it. They did a very thorough job entering most of the businesses, asking everyone if they had noticed their friend walking around.

But they came up empty.

*****

They found Chance's body in the early afternoon. Zeke was returning some empty gas containers to the barn and saw Chance hanging from one of the beams. There was a slip of paper in his

231

front pants pocket with a hand scrawled message that read –

I'm sorry!

Zeke brought the men to the barn to disclose his discovery. Michaels looked away when he saw his friend dangling above the ground like a masterless marionette.

"Jesus Christ," he said. "Somebody cut him down already."

"We can't," Strickler said. "Even redneck police don't want their crime scenes muddied."

"Fuck the police," Michaels said. "Fuck the police and fuck this place."

Quinlan studied Chance, making some notes in a pad. Michaels saw this and slapped the pad out of his hand and onto the ground. Quinlan remained calm. He bent down and retrieved the paper and pen.

"And fuck you," Michaels said to Quinlan. "That's our friend there."

"I'm simply making a note," he said stiffly to Michaels. "For the will. There are only two contestants left. That needs to be altered in all of the papers."

"Listen to me, you heartless prick. He wasn't a contestant," Michaels said. "He was a person. We – we are people."

"No one is saying you're not," Quinlan said. "But to be blunt, I do not care about your humanity.

I am only here to administer the game and record the results and bestow the winnings."

"You son-of-a-bitch…"

Strickler grabbed Michaels arm to stop him from stepping up on the lawyer.

"Lay off, Bernie."

"Whatever."

Michaels shook his arm free and stormed out of the barn. Strickler studied Chance's corpse. Judging from the shallow drop, the neck didn't break, which means his friend suffocated, dying slowly of brain ischemia, an even more painful death. Turning, something caught Strickler's eye. He walked over to where a bottle of bourbon lay on its side, with a little of the brown liquor still inside.

"What are you looking at, Doctor?" Quinlan asked. "What is it you see?"

Strickler turned to the lawyer.

"Bourbon," he said. "I didn't think that was Ethan's preferred drink."

*****

After examining the body and taking photographs of the scene, Darryl the Medical Examiner cut it down. With help from an attendant and Zeke, Chance was laid out on a gurney and covered with a sheet. Sheriff Waters played with the toothpick in his mouth, moving it from side to side.

"What do you think of this, Darryl? Two deaths in a span of two days. Both suicides? That just seems a bit far-fetched, don't it?"

"I only know about time and mode of death, Sheriff. What that means is up to you."

"Yeah it is, isn't it? Lucky me." the Sherriff said. "So? What do you have for me?"

"My official report will be done after the autopsy, but yeah, strangulation was the cause of death."

With that, Darryl and his attendant wheeled the copse out of the barn.

Waters sighed. He looked over at Zeke who had removed a pouch of chewing tobacco from his overalls and was stuffing a big pinch in his mouth.

"They back at the house?"

Zeke spit a wad of juice.

"In the den," he said.

Waters shook his head and headed toward the house. He never liked city people and the tourists that flocked their town when leaves turned colors. He found them pushy, needy, and just overall pains-in-the-asses.

These men took the fucking cake of assholes.

*****

"Now this is a sleepy town. People tend to die of natural causes in these parts. Cancer, heart attacks, those kinds of things. Now I have two stiffs over the course of twenty-four hours. That tends to raise eyebrows, you understand."

Michaels and Strickler sat side-by-side on the sofa. They watched the Sheriff pace the floor in front of them. Quinlan sat in large overstuffed chair, sipping tea.

"Truly an unfortunate coincidence, Sherriff," Quinlan said.

Waters shot Quinlan a nasty look.

"That was my polite talk," he said gruffly. "Now let me get to the straight-fucking-point. I've done my civic duty and done some checking. Seems like this Farnsworth character was used to getting his own way. Arranging all that stuff around here with the mayor."

"To which the town was handsomely compensated," Quinlan interjected.

"A big shot used to having his money do his muscle work. You handle that for him too?"

"I arrange all types of services for my clients," Quinlan replied evasively.

"Which is lawyer-talk for bullshit. But money or no money, we have two – let's call them – "out of the ordinary" deaths –"

"A coincidence," Quinlan interjected again.

"Maybe… But I've been around the block once or twice and two suicides happening at the same place and in such short of time, well sir, that dog just don't hunt."

"For what it's worth, it's well-documented that suicide rates are highest among adults between the ages of 45 and 64."

"Oh, is that a fact? Just had that little statistic at your fingertips, did you?"

"It's not a crime to be well-read."

"Not yet," said the Sheriff. "But the way things are going around here, maybe it should be."

Quinlan set down his cup and sighed. "What will you have us do, Sheriff?"

Waters held up his notebook.

"Don't be in a rush to leave our local hospitality just yet. If I have additional questions – and I will have them rest assured about that – or need to follow up on your statements, you'll oblige me I suspect."

"Without hesitation," Quinlan said.

Waters looked at the lawyer.

"You represent those fellows?" he asked.

"No, Sheriff. They are not my clients. Do they need counsel?"

"Good. Then do me a favor and let them answer my damn question. You boys going to stick around, yeah?"

Michaels and Strickler answered in unison.

"Yes."

"Good," Waters said. He headed for the door. He addressed the room before leaving. "Oh, one more thing. I'd keep a sharp eye out for each other if I were you."

"Why's that?" Strickler asked.

"You know, in case another," Waters said turning toward Quinlan. "How'd you put it? Oh, yeah, in case another 'coincidence' happens."

*****

Michaels smoked a cigarette on the porch when Strickler walked out. The two men leaned against the railing looking out at the hills in the distance.

"Is there someone we can call?" Michaels asked.

"Call? For what?" Strickler said.

"Chance is dead, Ted," Michaels said. "Doesn't he have a relative or next-of-kin or something like that?"

"Beats me."

"That's depressing," Michaels said. "Isn't that depressing? How do we not know if a person we've known since were in our late teens doesn't have a significant other or offspring or even a distant cousin. He was an only child, I remember that."

"Just us," Strickler said. "He just had us. If bad luck didn't exist, then Ethan would have had no luck at all."

"That's not funny," Michaels said.

"I wasn't trying to be," Strickler replied. "I was making a point."

"And what point was that?"

"That if this group was the closest thing he had to family, no wonder the poor bastard killed himself."

Michaels ruminated on this.

"It doesn't make sense. Things might be bad but nothing's *that* bad. The Sheriff has a point. Two suicides back-to-back like that? There's just too much coincidence."

"I don't know. Let's see, he suffered guilt... anger...embarrassment... Some combination of all three. Who knows, maybe he killed Farnsworth and then killed himself. No one has explored that option yet."

"Jesus, Ted. Show some respect for the dead."

"For who – Ethan or Farnsworth?"

"Ethan wouldn't hurt a fly."

"You say so, but it's been a long time since any of us has seen each other. Lots of things happen in those years. Who's to say? It's just a hypothesis. You're the one that said two suicides seemed too improbable."

"Yeah, but by that logic, how do I know that you didn't kill Farnsworth?"

"Right. And how do I know that you didn't?"

"Because I know what I did and did not do."

"So do I, but here we are just the same." Strickler paused before he brought up his next point. "You know what was found next to Chance's body? A nearly empty bottle of bourbon. You like bourbon, don't you, Bernie? Did you have a drink with Ethan last night...?"

"I don't like what you're implying," Michaels said.

"Yeah? Well, I'll tell you what I don't like – that lawyer. Have you noticed he is the only person that doesn't seem surprised about what's going on here?"

Michaels considered that a moment. Strickler had a point. Quinlan didn't seem phased at all when Chance's body was found, and he handled the interchange with the sheriff like it was old hat. Yeah, something was funny with that guy.

"He was the one that said Farnworth was murdered. Maybe we should have a talk with him," Michaels said.

*****

They found Quinlan in the game room, shifting through a neat stack of legal papers. When the men entered, Quinlan looked up and smiled. He removed his reading glasses and set them aside.

"Gentlemen, an unexpected pleasure."

"Can the formalities," Michaels said. "We want answers."

"Answers? I'm not sure what you mean."

"Come on, Quinlan. We want to know what's going on," Strickler said.

"I'm still not following."

"You come to town and everything gets fucked up," Michaels said. "People are dead."

"I came to town *after* Mr. Farnsworth passed," Quinlan corrected.

"You said he was murdered," Strickler said.

"Am I wrong?" Quinlan asked. His tone was light and condescending.

"The medical examiner said it was suicide," Strickler said.

"Then why are you here?" the lawyer asked.

"We want you to pull the plug on the game," Michaels said. "At least until all of this sorts out."

"I would advise against that," Quinlan said. "Breach of the agreement will find you in a massive lawsuit of which you have no hope of winning."

Michaels barked out a laugh.

"Joke's on you. I have no money to take."

"Money, no. But property, savings, retirement, anything remaining that you or your family has of value…"

"You'd go after my family, you son-of-a-bitch?"

Quinlan's face got very serious. He stared intently into Michaels' eyes so that there was little chance of misunderstanding.

"Be assured of it." Quinlan's words were cold and measured.

"You're sick," Strickler said.

"I'm carrying out the late wishes of my client. That's my job. Your job is to play the game that you started. That is all."

"Two people are dead," Michaels said.

"So, you've said. And the only bearing that has on the game is that there is one less person standing in your way to the prize."

Strickler shook his head.

"The Sheriff's right. Something's not adding up."

"I've found that very few things in life 'add up'. Maybe the course of events has been different in your personal lives," Quinlan remarked.

The remark stung with its precision and accuracy. In an instant their advantage was neutralized, and the men found themselves trying to get back on even ground. Quinlan stood up.

"You think something's amiss? Perhaps you are right. But if something is, it's not an orchestration of mine."

"Then whose is it?" Michaels asked.

"Examine the evidence. Fact: two deaths, explainable although highly improbable, occur within 24 hours of each other. Fact: one of you expects to inherit an obscene amount of money. Fact…"

"What are you suggesting?" Strickler interrupted.

The lawyer turned to Strickler and gave the doctor the slightest of smirks.

"Doctor, why make me say when it's on the tips of both your tongues? If you believe that one or both of their lives were terminated and not the result of their own machinations, then it only makes sense that one of you is the murderer. You two are the only ones to materially and perhaps even emotionally profit from the removal of everyone else."

The statement was a dump of cold water on the men's faces.

"That's ridiculous!" Strickler proclaimed. "I'll sue you for libel and defamation of character and anything else that's relevant."

"I didn't kill anyone!" Michaels protested.

"Motive is damning evidence. Who else stands to benefit an eight-billion-dollar windfall? My name is not on the contract. Both of yours are. If you're looking for the wolf among the sheep, so to speak, look no further than each other."

Michaels and Strickler exchanged suspicious glances. Quinlan was firmly in charge.

"Play the game, gentlemen. Play the game and fulfill your obligation."

Quinlan walked in between the men toward the exit. He paused by a framed needlepoint hanging on the wall. It read:

"The Lord takes care of His own."

"A religious man, Mr. Boyle," he said.

"Boyle? Who the hell is that?" Strickler asked.

"I believe his Christian name is Zeke."

"I never knew his last name," Michaels said.

"You never asked," countered Quinlan. "How do you expect to win a game based on intuition and perception when you're neither inquisitive nor observant? See you tonight, gentlemen. Eight o'clock sharp."

Quinlan left the two men alone. The atmosphere had noticeably changed; long held animosity shared between the two old friends had turned into outright suspicion and distrust.

One of them a murderer?

Was that really possible?

"I'm going to take a nap," Michaels said.

"Yeah," Strickler said. "That's a good idea."

The two of them went upstairs in a silent procession.

Chapter 12

In his room, Strickler dumped the contents of his medical bag out on the bed. The two vials of Fentanyl cascaded down on the quilt. The small vials were empty. His drug had run dry.

"Dammit," he muttered. He checked the clock. It was four o'clock. Four hours until the game was on. Plenty of time to chip, if he had something to chip with.

He stormed out of this bedroom and headed down the stairs. He checked for Zeke but couldn't find the old farmer anywhere. Strickler swore under his breath and then noticed the old man's truck keys on the counter near the sink.

"Zeke," he said aloud to no one in particular. "I'm going to borrow the truck for a bit, okay?"

He didn't wait for a response he never expected. He rushed out the front door and to the truck in the driveway.

Zeke stared out a window in his room and watched the doctor climb into his truck. He rubbed his chin with his hand. His expression was tough to read; like a frog, he just stared at the fly without indication of what he was thinking or what he was feeling until his tongue shot out, bringing his squirming victim to his mouth.

*****

The pharmacist in town was a fresh face right out of pharmacy school. He had a high and tight haircut and his face didn't look like it had ever needed to see the edge of a razor. Strickler rapped his fingers on the counter as the pharmacist unlocked a cabinet and looked through the various medications.

"We got all sorts… Percocet, Codeine, liquid Nemenol…"

"Fentanyl," Strickler said quickly, putting his medical license back into his wallet. He caught himself and said in a more measured voice, "I need Fentanyl."

The young pharmacist slowly looked up at Strickler.

"That's powerful stuff," he said.

"I'm well aware of the potency."

The pharmacist scrutinized Strickler then sighed. He removed a familiar small vial from the cabinet.

"Be careful. Never more than 2 milligrams. Sure, as all get-out, that'll put you in a coma the likes of which you might not wake up from."

Strickler set his credit card on the counter.

"I'm a physician," he said. "I'm always careful."

*****

Michaels removed the revolver from his dresser drawer. He brandished it like a tough guy, admiring his reflection in the mirror. In the wake of lawyer's talk, he was glad that he had it. So small and yet so deadly. He felt powerful with it in his hand.

Michaels looked over at the bathroom door. He tucked the gun into his waist band of his pants and walked into the bathroom and to the door adjoined to Strickler's room. He bent down and peered through the keyhole.

From his vantage, Strickler was not there. He opened the door carefully, just in case Strickler was lurking outside the keyhole's perspective. The room was messier than he had anticipated, a towel on the ground, a jacket collapsed on the floor. His bed looked like his medical bag had thrown up on it.

Michaels' attention immediately was drawn to the two vials lying on their side on the night table. He picked one up, and then saw the syringe case.

Suspicion of the doctor's continued use of opiates confirmed, Michaels retreated to his room, bracing a chair underneath the doorknob. Drugs made people dangerous. Users in need of a fix were often unpredictable and subject to severe and extreme violence.

It was good that he had a gun, Michaels thought. It was too bad that he didn't know the identity of his benefactor. He would have liked to give him a sincere "thank you".

*****

At the base of the stairs, the large Grandfather clock's little hand was fixed on the "8" and the big hand clicked the "12." The gongs that reverberated in the still house were a loud reminder that the men were being summoned, that from somewhere from the great beyond, Farnsworth was requesting their presence forthwith.

In his room, Michaels ground out his cigarette. The ashtray had been made from a child's hands – crude clay coils painted and hardened in a kiln. He stood and pulled over the hoodie, tucking it down over his waist. He checked his reflection in the mirror to make sure the gun-butt was covered, then he exited the room.

Strickler was uncharacteristically wired. Normally cool, the doctor paced up and down the small room since he had returned from his shopping trip. He had expected Zeke to rip him a new one, but the old man didn't utter a word. He accepted the keys back with a hospitable nod and then went about this business without a word.

Strickler inserted a syringe into the Fentanyl vial and filled it. He then tucked the syringe into his coat pocket before heading out the door.

Quinlan stood in the game room waiting for the two contestants. On the table, the last manila envelope lay ready for the final disclosure.

Michaels entered first with Strickler close behind.

"We're here," said Michaels.

Quinlan turned to face the men. He smiled broadly and nodded his head.

"The final clue. You are at the end of your journey, gentlemen."

"Secrets can be smothering," Michaels said.

"Perceptive," Quinlan said. "Are you ready?

"Let's get this over with," Strickler said.

Both men had enough of this ceremony. Quinlan consented to their wishes, picking up the envelope and turning it over to the item fell out. It clanged on the glass top of the table.

"What's that?" Strickler frowned.

"A bracelet. A child's ID bracelet. The kind that would have a name inscribed on it. Like Brenda or Brittany."

Strickler picked up the bracelet and noticed a tag on it. It had two sets of numbers:

13   23

He offered it to Michaels who turned it over in his fingers. He bore a similar puzzled expression.

"How exciting to be on the verge of the greatest discovery of your lives," Quinlan said. "I envy you."

"This isn't exactly stepping foot in the new world, but I get you," Michaels said.

"With all due respect to Columbus, the fortune he received for bringing back livestock and tobacco to the Queen of Spain pale in comparison to the spoils to winner of this game. By this time tomorrow, one of you will go from a no one to being in the *Who's Who of Business*. Any questions before we begin?"

"One," Strickler said. "Something you suggested before got me thinking. If you think that one of us killed Farnsworth or Ethan, how come you're not worried that you might not be next on the list?"

Never betraying his cool, Quinlan smiled.

"I never said one of you *was* the killer, Doctor," he said. "I only helped articulate what was already fermenting in your minds. What you yourselves were intimating but too fearful to express. Are you a killer? Is Mr. Michaels? That's not my business. This is."

He took the ID bracelet from Michaels' hands and held it out to both men.

"Now," he said. "You're wasting valuable time."

*****

It was an odd position to be in, having to rely on your opponent for success as he had to rely on yours, Strickler thought. The challenge was going to be taking advantage of a moment, getting that head-start, cutting the right corner. For a drunk fool, he couldn't afford to underestimate Michaels. Not at this juncture. He stared at Michaels too long because when he turned from the side window, he made direct eye contact with Strickler.

"What are you staring at?"

"I was just thinking. An ID bracelet with a redemption tag. I saw a jewelry store last night. It can't be that easy, can it?"

"It isn't yet."

A pause.

"What the lawyer said," Strickler said after the silence grew too awkward. "What do you think? Is he right? Is one of us a killer?"

Michaels shrugged.

"I don't know, Ted. I wish to hell I did. I do know one thing though. Nothing is as it appears to be. There's so much misinformation and double talk I don't know what to think anymore."

It was a sincere admission devoid of any animosity. Strickler said nothing and nodded.

"You know," he said finally after a few moments had passed. "I hated you throughout college."

"Yeah, I know."

"Even when I saw you at the train station the other day. I was like, 'God, there he is'. And all those hateful memories came flooding back. Two days later, we're all that's left. And it suddenly dawned on me."

"What's that?"

"The person I've hated most of my life is now the only friend I have," Strickler said.

Zeke watched the men via the rearview mirror. They sat very far from one another trying to create as much space between them. The two men had been fighting like cats and dogs since they got there. And now it appeared that they had found a temporary détente. Zeke wondered which one would win a bare-knuckle, no-holds barred fight. He doubted if either of them had thrown a punch no less been on the receiving end of one. And in Zeke's perception, these were not men at all; they were just older versions of their college selves unable to shed the cocoons of their privileged existences.

Zeke let out a grunt and shook his head.

"Did you say something?" Strickler asked Zeke.

"No, sir," Zeke replied. "Just thought of something funny."

"Care to share it? I think we all could go for a good laugh right about now."

"What's the last thing you usually hear before a redneck dies?

"I don't know. What?"

"Hey y'all... watch this!"

Zeke laughed a bit too loudly, and too robustly. Strickler and Michaels exchanged a disconcerting look. Zeke quiet or Zeke boisterous, neither sat well with them.

*****

The sign read: "East Bumfuck Jewelry". Michaels banged on the window to get the attention of an old man who was puttering around the front counter. The old man looked up and shook his head, pointing to his watch as if to say, "the store is closed".

"Offer him something," Michaels said.

"Like what?"

"You got cash?"

"I do now – don't you?"

Michaels dug into his pocket and came up with a bankcard.

"Really?" Strickler muttered. "Not even walking around money?"

"Who carries bills anymore?" Michaels said.

Strickler removed his wallet and removed a hundred-dollar bill and plastered it against the window. The old man's eyes perked up and he waddled over to the door, unlocking it, and poked his head through.

"What you want?" he asked.

"We need to ask you a question about this?" Strickler said. He held up the ID bracelet.

"Come back tomorrow. We're open at nine a.m."

"A hundred bucks to answer a couple of questions. That's not a bad profit for ten minutes of your time."

The old man considered. He snatched the bill from Strickler and opened the door for the two men to come inside. The old man went to the counter and turned on the magnifying lamp. He regarded the bracelet, turning it over in his hands.

"Sorry," the old man said. "I don't recognize it."

"Please, this is important. Can you check the tag?"

The old man sighed. He looked at the tag and went to the wall where merchandise ready to pick-up was stored. He ran a finger against the numbers on the drawers.

"Well, I'll be a son-of-a-bitch..." he said.

He found a drawer labeled 1323. He opened it. Inside there was a sealed envelope. He handed it over and Strickler snatched it from his hand. He tore it open and pulled out a letter.

"What's it say?" Michaels asked.

Strickler's face deflated. He handed over the paper to Michaels and walked out the front door. Michaels lowered the page and placed it on the counter.

"Thanks," he said to the old man and followed Strickler outside.

The note was short and to the point:

"Something about endings can be so satisfying...
This is not one of those."

Michaels lit a cigarette. The exasperation welling inside him shook his hand. After the third unsuccessful attempt of lighting it, he tossed the cigarette aside.

"Alright. What are we going to do now?" he said.

"We keep looking. What else can we do?"

"Where? We can't just go running around town like we did last night. We got lucky. I don't think we're going to get lucky twice."

"What do you want me to say, Bernie? 'We'll figure it out'? Everything's going to be fine'? I can't say that because I don't know that."

"I wish Chance were here," Michaels said. "He could work out problems like this."

"I'm not dumb," Strickler said.

"I didn't say you were," Michaels replied. "I'm just saying he was – I don't know – creative. A creative thinker. We aren't."

"You're an asshole."

"What's your problem?"

"This!" Strickler held up the ID bracelet. "And this!" he gestured to the surrounding environment. He then looked up at the sky. "And that son-of-a-bitch up there. You hear me, Farnsworth? You're a son-of-a-bitch!"

"Take it easy, Ted. That's not going to solve anything."

Strickler turned to Michaels.

"Do you know why Farnsworth kept you around, Bernie? You were a kicked-around puppy to him. Something to be nurtured and tortured and nurtured again. And like any other lapdog, you kept coming back for more, unable to understand that the hand he fed from and the hand that slapped him were one in the same."

Michaels' face flushed red with anger. He grabbed Strickler by the jacket lapels and rushed him against the brick wall of the building. The collision made a dull thud. Strickler used his elbow to pry one of Michaels' arms loose, and once he did, he drove the elbow into Michaels' sternum. A rush of air escaped from Michaels' lungs as he stood fighting for breath. Strickler grabbed him in a headlock, intent on choking his friend out. Michaels fought for air, his eyes wide and glassy and helpless. His hand started to reach for the gun in the front pouch of his sweatshirt, when headlights from a car beamed on them. A truck drove past, the driver laying on his horn to break up or cheer on the fight. It pulled over to the side of the road across from the combatants. Two burly men got out of the truck and opened the door to the truck bed.

Strickler let Michaels go. Michaels collapsed onto his knees fighting to get his breath back.

"Jesus, Ted," Michaels croaked. "What's the matter with you? You almost killed me."

Strickler regained his composure, reflexively smoothing out his attire.

"Look," he said. "I'm sorry. Let's just solve this thing and get out of here."

Michaels nodded. He slowly got to his feet and dug into his pocket to withdraw the bracelet.

"These numbers, what could they be?" Michaels said, rubbing his throat.

"Who knows? They could be anything."

"So, shout out anything."

"A street address maybe."

"Part of a phone number."

"A PIN?" Strickler offered.

"Do people around here look like they use PINs?"

Michaels distracted himself by watching the pick-up truck workers lift large bulky items and load them into the back of the truck. They were heavy and with each load the truck bed sagged under the weight. Curious, Michaels stared at the men. He slowly drifted to the street curb.

"Where are you going?"

Michaels didn't answer him. Instead, he crossed the street and stood in front of East Bumfuck Granite and Marble. There, he watched the workers lift newly cut graveyard headstones.

Strickler didn't get it. He followed Michaels across the street.

"What are you doing?" he asked.

Michaels didn't immediately answer. His eyes were focused on something that Stickler either couldn't see or didn't understand.

"Look at that," Michaels said. He pointed at the face of one of the headstones. The name plate was blank and shiny just like the face of the bracelet. Strickler stared for a moment before it sunk in.

"Son-of-a-bitch," he said. "Let me see that thing."

Michaels handed him over the bracelet. Strickler looked at the clear plate of the bracelet and then at the clear name plate of the headstone.

"You think this is it?" he asked Michaels.

"It has to be."

"Then that would make 13-23 coordinates on a map?"

"Or a cemetery," Michaels said.

*****

If "small-town New England cemetery" was an entry in the encyclopedia, the East Bumfuck cemetery would be the accompanying photo insert. Black wrought-iron fencing and a crumbling stone wall loosely wrapped around an uneven field of very old gravestones. A dense line of northern hardwood trees provided a wide canopy shielding the cemetery from the light of the stars and the moon. Further obscuring visibility, a late-night fog misted over the cemetery as the approaching cold collided with the humidity and ultimately settling uniformly over the ground.

Michaels and Strickler stood at the front gate. The door had long been broken, hanging askew and barely clinging to the rusty hinge at the top, a victim of years of neglect and lack of municipal refurbishment funds. The cemetery was wider than it was long; the rows of headstones laying east-to-west within its fractured boundaries seemed limitless.

Even though neither would admit it, fear gripped them both firmly. Graveyards inspired fear in anyone, especially at night, when the silence was deafening, and people shuddered in expectation of the unknown.

"I hate cemeteries," Michaels said. "Christ, when did it get so fucking cold?" He instinctively felt for the reassuring bump of the gun in his hoodie front pocket.

When he turned to answer him, Strickler saw the gun butt poking out of the hoodie front pouch before Michaels pushed it back deeper. He looked away quickly not to let on. Knowing Michaels carried heat made the hairs on the back of his neck stand on end, and he did his best to stay focused. Besides, his own hand found the syringe full of Fentanyl in his jacket pocket, his own ace in the hole.

Strickler apprehensively surveyed the cemetery.

"You know what the general rule about cemeteries is, don't you, Bern'?"

"No, what's that?"

"'Don't be buried first, and sure as hell don't be buried last.'"

"I'll be sure to remember that."

The men clicked on their penlights and began to creep slowly and quietly down the staggered rows of graves. There was an initial attempt to keep the rows tight and in some order, but that attention to detail was lost somewhere between the late-1800s and early twentieth century. The rest of the graves had been sporadically placed, sometimes in line with existing markers, other times they were interred depending on the natural limiting contours of the surrounding environment.

The penlights shone on names like Franklin, Fletcher, Bailey, and Sheldon with dates as early as 1825 and as recent as 2013. Michaels watched Strickler walk across some graves.

"Don't walk on a grave," warned Michaels. "Bad luck."

"That's 'walk over' a grave," Strickler corrected. "You know, like, you look like someone just walked over your grave." Then he pointed at Michaels. "Kind of what you're doing."

Bernie looked down.

"Shit, you serious?"

"Look over there, see if you find any markers," Strickler said.

Michaels searched the grass. In some areas he had to use his toe to nudge around looking for the row marker. The groundskeeper did a poor job of edging, and in some places where large tufts of grass and weeds grew, flat-out ignored trimming. After beating down the overgrowth with his foot, Michaels' toe-prodding hit against something solid.

"I think I have something here," he said. Michaels got on one knee and used his hands to pull away thick grass. Strickler raced over, standing behind him shining the light down. Michaels' fingernails scraped back tufts of crab grass and dirt to reveal an old stone with some etchings in it.

"It's a marker," he said. "I got a marker."

"And? Spit it out."

Michaels squinted, wiping the dirt away with the side of his hand.

"35-30."

Strickler ran to the next row. He got on his hands and knees and furiously scraped away the overgrowth until his fingers unearthed that row's stone marker.

"23-19," he said. "This way."

Michaels scrambled to his feet and ran over to the last row on the other side of Strickler. It was his turn to dig and report.

"19-30."

Strickler looked around. He sprinted over to newer area of the cemetery that had been separated by an above-ground crypt. He fell to his knees frantically excavating until he found the worn marker.

"17-06."

The men shared a look. In unison they ran to the next row. Michaels got there first, digging in the dirt like junkyard dog after a bone. He dug so hard that he nearly tore off the nails on the index fingers on both hands. He nodded at Strickler after he uncovered the marker

"This is it," he said.

Together, the men walked down to a headstone. It was considerably newer than the ones surrounding it, as was the dirt that had covered the grave. The newly-etched marble face of the headstone featured a blank shiny nameplate. The men searched around the grave looking for an object or another clue that would lead them to the object. They came up empty.

"What are we supposed to do now?" Michaels asked.

Something caught Strickler's eye. A gravedigger's shovel leaned against a nearby headstone. He walked over and grabbed it in his hand. Regardless if it was purposefully left there for the men or a coincidence, he knew what had to be done.

"The only thing we can do," Strickler said. "We dig."

*****

Digging a grave took a lot of muscle. But digging up an already dug grave required courage as well as strength. The dirt was fortunately moist, but that only meant the soil was rich and heavy. The lights from both penlights provided a tease of visibility and lack of water made the men's thirst burn more intensely. They traded off when the other man tired. Taking turns not only made the job easier, but it was an investment both made to ensure the integrity of the game. Both had expelled equal physical effort in uncovering the object.

Michaels was in the trench when his shovel hit something solid that wasn't a rock. He drove the shovel against the object again to reaffirm this revelation.

"I got something here," he said.

Strickler jumped in the hole and helped Michaels clear the soil until it exposed the Mahogany wood face of the casket. The two men paused, catching their breath.

"Open it," Strickler said.

"What if there's a body in there? Like a real body?"

"It's a game, Bernie. Nothing's real," Strickler said. "Farnsworth's not going to make us dig up a real corpse. That would be illegal."

"Take a look around," Michaels said. "This cemetery is pretty real."

"I'll do it."

Strickler grabbed the shovel out of Michaels hand. He used the head as a wedge to pry open the lid.

"Give me a hand," Strickler said through gritted teeth. Reluctantly, Michaels grabbed part of the shovel's handle and pulled down hard with Strickler until the lid started moving.

"Almost there," Strickler said.

Behind them, a muffled noise sounded. A voice? Michaels turned.

"Who's there?" he asked.

No one responded. They didn't have to. If the penlights were brighter, Michaels might have seen the figure lurking behind them, or seen its long shadow cast across the ground. But as it was, the trees blocked out the starlight, and by the time he saw the baseball bat coming at his head, it was too late.

*****

When Michaels opened his eyes, he still saw the stars that had first sent him on this journey into the dark. The more he moved, the more pain shot through his head. That was a good sign; feeling nothing would have meant he had likely passed on to the next world. Whoever swung the baseball bat didn't want him dead; he wanted him taken out of the picture. Score one for the Louisville Slugger.

When his eyes got reacquainted with the living world, he found himself laying on the side of the dug-up grave. He struggled to get himself on his elbows but was suddenly pushed back down by the shovel head.

"Why don't you set a spell, Mr. Michaels," a familiar voice said. "I'm still waiting to see if the doctor is going to wake up."

Michaels saw Strickler's motionless body on the other side of the grave.

"What did you do with Ted?"

"Nothing that I didn't do to you. Well, maybe I did crack him a bit harder. I never cared much for the doctor. Grated on my nerves."

"Who are you telling?" Michaels mumbled.

"But he got better than some people got. Some people just don't have a chance in the world. Anyway, asleep or dead, it don't matter to me. I just needed one of you alive."

"Why just one of us alive?" Michaels' voice trailed off. He looked at the old man. His face stared solemnly at the coffin. Maybe it was the way he looked, the way his normally hard eyes were soft and vulnerable. Whatever it was, it struck Michaels' heart and his eyes suddenly went wide. He knew whose grave they this was.

"Oh my God," he said. "This is your daughter's grave, isn't it?

Zeke looked at him through eyes that had seen their share of tears that had all been cried out.

"Yes sir," he said without hint of emotion.

"Look, we didn't know it was her grave. The clue brought us here. The numbers on the bracelet and the marker. We just made a mistake. A bad one. We thought it was just part of the game, not a real grave."

Zeke smiled sardonically and shook his head.

"You still don't get it, do you? Your mind just can't wrap around it all."

"You hit me pretty hard. I'm a bit slow."

"Your friend understood. I thought he was crazy when he first approached me with his idea. I almost hit him in the head, if you want to know the truth of it. But I could tell he wanted to do something. He wanted to do the right thing. That's why you all are here."

"Are you talking about Farnsworth? What about Farnsworth?"

"I'm seventy-seven years old, Mr. Michaels. My daughter Alison would have been fifty-eight years old next week. She was our only child. Precious the way little girls are supposed to be but friendly and smart as a whip."

As he talked, Zeke checked to see if Strickler was still breathing. He kept the head of the shovel pointed menacingly at Michaels, a not-so-pleasant reminder to heed his directions or suffer the consequences.

"You have any children, Mr. Michaels?"

"Two girls."

"Then you ought to know. Man has a daughter, there ain't nothing he won't do for her. He promises to tuck her in every night and take her to school every morning. You provide for her, make sure she has every opportunity at her fingertips because she's the best part of you. So, when she says she wants to go to college out of state, well, what father whose been saving every single penny and spare dime for eighteen years can say 'no' tothat?"

"They make life worth it."

"You say you got two daughters. Can you imagine how it might feel if someone robbed one of them of their life?"

"Your daughter was killed?"

"Yes, sir. When she got to college. Killed in a cemetery of all places. A cemetery…" Zeke had to look away to compose himself.

A sickening feeling took root in Michaels' stomach and steadily spread throughout his body. *A cemetery. A college. A dead girl.* These words thumped with the resonance of a hammer's strike on the head of nail. His mouth suddenly got very dry, making his voice sound raspy.

"What college?"

"She was the apple of my eye, Mr. Michaels. All children are fragile, but a daughter's special. The moment she is born, you swear to cherish and protect her. You make that promise. You make that commitment. And she counts on it."

"What college was it?" Michaels asked again. The sickening feeling had turned into a heavy ice ball in the pit of his stomach.

"Why her? That's what I want to know. What me and the missus always wanted to know. Who decides that this person or that person looks like a good victim? What kind of person acts on it?"

Michaels was overwhelmed. His head throbbed; he could feel the blood pushing against the veins in his temples. He looked away from Zeke's eyes. They were surprisingly neither angry nor vengeful. They just held a look of someone needing to know the truth. Michaels vomited on the ground.

"It was an accident," he said, wiping his mouth with the back of his hand. "It was Saint Patrick's Day. We had been drinking all day and it was late. We stopped at a gas station for some gas. There was a local there giving a pretty girl a hard time. We didn't know her, but knew she went to the college. You didn't forget who the first girls admitted to your all-boy's college. So, we stopped him, and the girl took off. The walk back up to campus was a tough trek sober, but impossible when you were drunk. She cut through the cemetery. Someone said we should follow her, so we decided to follow her."

Alison didn't feel well. She entered the old Jesuit cemetery to get away from the creep at the gas station. Walking had become a difficult task. Why did she drink so much?

"You followed her? Zeke asked prodding Michaels with the shovel. "Why?"

Michaels swallowed hard.

"To have fun," he said weakly.

"To have fun? And just how exactly were you going to have fun with her?" Zeke pressed him.

"I wish I could say we went after her for noble purposes."

Alison sat on a large headstone to stop the dizziness that blurred her mind. She didn't see the car in the street drive by, stop, and back up. She didn't hear the doors open and shut or the four figures that exited the car headed to the cemetery gates. Once inside, they dispersed, going after their target from different directions.

Alison got to her feet and searched for the path that led up the hill to the school. Suddenly, she heard sounds around her – footsteps. People's voices. She shook her head to try to clear it. She saw shadows moving around, surrounding her. Fear spiked through her body.

More rustling and she took off. She might have made it to the path, but she ran smack-dab into a headstone, sending her flying to the ground. The biology textbook landed a few feet away.

A set of hands found her. They belonged to Michaels, who stood over her trying to get her to her feet. He grabbed her wrists. Alison fought, flailing her arms. The struggle causes her ID bracelet's clasp to break and fall on the ground.

"Go away!" She yelled. It came out incoherent.

When the figure laughed, she kicked her way to her feet and tried to bolt. She ran into Chance who barely held onto her without being knocked over. Strickler grabbed her from behind and tossed her on the ground. She hit it hard enough to temporarily lose her breath. She fought to get back her air.

Michaels, Strickler, Chance, and Farnsworth stood over her. Four seniors who wanted to finish their final year of college with something memorable. Their faces were primal, lurid, and carnal.

Their intention was clear.

The men's hands ravaged her body. Squeezing. Rubbing. Feeling.

Survival. That was the only thought coursing through Alison's mind. Survival. Enduring this assault and coming out on the other side.

Someone tore her white blouse shirt.

Someone yanked her bra away from her breasts.

Someone's hands delved under her skirt.

The fingers that invaded her privates were cold.

Tears rolled down her face.

"No-no-no-no-no..."

Alison fought to keep focus. She had to keep her thoughts clear. She summoned her strength and when the men fought for the right to grab an area on her body, she jumped at the chance to break through their fumbling.

She scrambled to her feet with the conviction of fight-or-flight necessity. She ran straight through Chance and Strickler. In the street, she saw drunken people walk by. She tried to scream and get their attention, but nothing came out.

"Come back here, bitch!" Strickler called.

269

She was gone in a full-tilt boogie. She tripped over a marker, stumbling to regain balance. Her arms pinwheeled for balance but she careened away, her head colliding into the spiked barb of a headstone shaped like a Fleury Cross.

The four friends gathered around her, watching the blood pool around her. The brilliance of her blue eyes that once saw the possibilities of the future in front of her steadily faded away.

A tear ran down Michaels' face.

"You just left her there," Zeke said. "Like a dog on the side of the road. You just left here like some diseased stray to die."

"We got out of there pretty quick. We were scared. We didn't intend for that to happen. It just did."

"No one felt bad about what they did? No one accept the fact that they did wrong?"

Michaels looked at the scar on his wrist. He just shook his head in response to Zeke's questions.

"Later, it was Farnsworth's idea to seal our secrecy in blood."

Farnsworth heated up a knife blade under a lighter.

"This is something that dies with the four people in this room. Is that understood? No one will speak of this now or ever. We are bounded by blood now. We are guardians of each other's secrets."

He sliced each of their wrists, and one by one, they pressed the cuts together, merging their blood.

Strickler's eyes fluttered open. He didn't move once he heard Michaels' voice speak of an incident that was sworn never to be spoken about again. He had kept his eyes shut and his breathing regular as he listened to Michaels relay the horrible truth of that night. Now, with the curtain lifted, he needed to know what the situation was. From his vantage point on the ground, Zeke had his back toward him as he addressed Michaels on the ground.

Michaels rubbed his wrist with his other hand. He felt oddly calm, with the forty-year-old weight lifted from his back. There was nothing left but to tell the unvarnished truth. Two out of the four responsible for that ignominious event had finally met their Maker, and were no doubt bartering the value of their souls in Final Judgement.

"I'm not the same person I was back then," Michaels continued. "I'm a different man now. I even tried going to med school for a while after that. I thought that maybe if I could save someone, anyone, it'd somehow begin to make up for my part. That it would mean something."

Although he didn't sob or sniffle, tears rolled down Zeke's cheeks. The old man tightly squeezed the shovel's handle in his big, scarred hands.

"You have to understand," Michaels said. "We never meant to kill your daughter. It was an accident."

"She has a name, goddammit!"

271

"Alison," Michaels said. "We never meant to kill Alison."

Strickler made a subtle move to catch Michaels' attention. Michaels glanced at Strickler in silent acknowledgement, then turned back to Zeke.

"Did you know who it was when you followed her? Did you know her then?"

"No. She was just there. It could have been anyone."

Strickler crawled slowly and quietly over to Zeke.

"Just like a bobcat on a woodchuck. You wanted to hurt something weaker than you. You picked the wrong child. You picked my child. You chose my Alison. You sons-of-bitches didn't even know her name. Well, now you do. And it's going to be the last name you're ever going to remember..."

Michaels went for the gun in his hoodie front pocket, but it wasn't there. He looked around the ground for it.

Zeke chuckled darkly.

"Imagine my surprise when this popped out of your sweatshirt when I hoisted you out of the grave. Didn't figure you for the type of person to pack a pistol. But then, I never figured you for a killer for that matter either."

Zeke leveled the .38 at Michaels.

"Why are you surprised? Didn't you put this in my room?"

"What are you talking about?"

"It's not mine. I found it in my drawer."

"And you think I put it there? You want to tell me why I'd want to put a weapon in the hands of a man I'm going to kill? That's just crazy. But now, it is for you. At least one of these bullets is."

Zeke pulled back the hammer. Michaels cringed.

Strickler let out a yell. Zeke turned in time to see Strickler stretch out and plunge the syringe in his hand deep into Zeke's leg. He depressed the plunger, emptying the contents into Zeke's body.

Zeke let out a howl. The surprise of the attack caught him off-guard, and the pain of a syringe plunged deep into his thigh muscle made him drop the gun.

"What's this?" Zeke asked, clutching his leg as he yanked the syringe out.

The impact of the drug hit him quickly. Zeke fell to one knee as the large quantities of the opiate coursed through the vein tributaries in his body. His breathing became irregular, his vision blurry.

"What did you do to me?" he wanted to say but only half the sentence was coherent. The rest was drowned out as froth started to form around his mouth. The old man fell onto his back, the momentum of his heavy frame carrying him into the grave. He landed on his daughter's coffin with a loud thud. His body twitched as it started to shut down one organ at a time.

"My sweet, sweet baby…" he croaked, as his breathing noticeably slowed. Foam started to flow from his mouth, and his eyes rolled back into his head. His brain shut down like an exhausted piece of equipment. In less than two minutes, he was dead.

Strickler got to his feet. He looked at the old man dead in the grave, then walked over and helped Michaels to his feet.

"You alright?" he asked him.

Michaels shook his head. The enormity of what had transpired still had him in its strangle hold and was reluctant to let go.

"I'm not okay, Ted," he said. "I haven't been okay for a long, long time."

"Shake it off."

"What are you saying? We *killed* a girl. You can't shake something like that off. You can bury it. You can repress it. But shake it off? How am I supposed to do that?"

"That was an accident. It's like you told him. We didn't go there to kill her. It just happened."

"You're right," Michaels said. "We didn't want to kill her. We just wanted to rape her."

"We made a mistake. One mistake doesn't a career criminal make. We would have gone to jail. Our lives would have turned out different."

Michaels looked up, hopeful.

"That sounds nice," he said. "Different would have been good."

"You think jail would have changed anything?"

"Maybe. Maybe I wouldn't have continued to hurt people like I've done. My wife or my kids. That alone would have been worth it. To not hurt anyone else."

"Get it together," Strickler said. "We have to find the object."

Michaels stared disbelievingly at the doctor.

"You think there's an object in that casket, Ted? You can't really believe that."

"I believe in the money. We signed the contract. That wasn't for show."

Michaels sighed. Strickler was so focused he failed to see the forest through the trees.

"You ever wonder why Farnsworth made us mingle blood that night?"

"For show. To make our promise to each other seem like it meant something. It didn't mean anything," Strickler was becoming agitated.

"No. He did it because the guilty are not supposed to forget. I mean, come on. We all tried to. How could we not? That's why we never saw each other all these years. The real reason. Because then we'd be forced to remember, and then we might have to talk about what we did."

Strickler saw the gun on the ground.

"So, what are you saying?" Strickler said. "The game was what – a joke? A way for Farnsworth to get a last dig in?"

275

Michaels turned his attention to the grave. He crouched down low, getting his hand on some dirt and tossing it into the hole.

"I don't think so. It was more of Farnsworth's way of making sure we didn't escape responsibility for what we did. It was his way to make it right. For him to do that, we all needed to be here. We needed to be a part of this."

Strickler bent down behind Michaels and picked up the .38.

"It was all in the name. It was there in front of our faces the entire time," Strickler said. "Chance knew it. He even told me."

"What do you mean?" Michaels' said, still looking at the coffin below that contained the last remains of a young girl whose death they had caused.

"Attrition," Strickler said. "You know what that means? Forced penance."

The sound of a gun being cocked behind Michaels did not surprise him. What surprise could top what he had just experienced? He turned slowly to see Strickler standing before him, the nickel-plated .38 pointed directly at him.

"What are you doing, Ted?"

"What's it look like? I'm finishing the game. Finishing what we started. We can't let Farnsworth down. Not now. We're so close. If you're not going to do it, then I damn sure am going to."

"It's over, Ted. This is the finish. This is the way Farnsworth wanted it and now it's over. The game was the lure to get us here, the money was to keep us here. There is no statute of limitations on murder."

"We didn't murder her. She fell. She died. End of story."

"That's not what I meant, and you know it."

Strickler smiled.

"Don't pull the sanctimonious bullshit act, Bernie. You haven't had the practice. I heard what you said to Zeke. 'Someone said we should follow her'. You remember who said it, don't you Bernie? You should. Those were your words. You saw her first at the gas station. Trying to be some white knight saving her from the evil townie. And all along, you just wanted to get inside her pants."

"Shut up," Michaels said.

"If we're going to air all our dirty laundry, then let's do it right. You wanted to do something to that poor girl."

"Alison," Michaels said.

"Kiss her, cop a feel, slide inside that young tight virgin…"

"Shut up!"

"Just making sure we both remember it right, Bernie. Accuracy of statement is important."

Michaels shook his head to clear the memory from his head.

"Shut up…" Michaels said, the guilt softening the rough edge of his voice.

"That's just like you, Bernie. Blaming all your failures on that one night. A guilty conscience didn't stop us from trying to rape that girl. It didn't derail our aspirations and dreams. Didn't derail us from having happy lives. It certainly didn't affect Farnsworth any. And it certainly didn't stop you from approaching Farnsworth for money all those years later."

"You're wrong, Ted."

"It doesn't matter. Now, stand up. Slowly."

Michaels grabbed a handful of dirt, as he stood up, and tossed some – but not all – into the desecrated grave.

"I didn't know. I didn't know what this was all about. Maybe I didn't want to know, just pushed it out of my mind. Maybe I hoped that Farnsworth just wanted to see us. There was a time we were friends. Before all the mental and emotional abuse. When we were just ourselves. I swear I remember it. Wasn't there?"

"Are you that dense? I knew it right from the beginning. I read the paper the next day. The rest of you put your heads in the sand. Farnsworth didn't, that's evident. I at least knew who she was. I knew her name."

Tears streamed down Michaels' cheeks. He could only manage a hoarse whisper in response.

"I didn't know."

"The other night I went to Farnsworth. I was going to tell him to go to hell. That I wasn't playing his stupid game for all the tea in China. But when I saw him, he was just sitting in the tub, without a care in the world. There was no guilt in his face, I can tell you that. He just remained the cocky king-in-exile even when I dropped the radio in the tub."

"You? It was you? You killed him?"

"Jesus, two days ago you were ready to do the job yourself. But I have to ask. Why did you bring the gun with you?"

"I didn't. It was in my drawer. Someone put it there. That and a flask of bourbon."

Stricker frowned. He wasn't expecting that.

"What is it?" Michaels asked.

"Someone put something in my drawer too."

"The drugs?"

Strickler shoots him a sharp look.

"How do you know? Was it you? Did you put it in there?"

"No," Michaels said. "But I saw the tracks the day after you used. Seems like someone was trying to bait us." Michaels paused. "My turn to have to ask a question. Did you kill Chance?"

"Chance figured out the game. Not right away, but he caught on. And when he had the opportunity to tell you or me about this find, well, let's just say he went with someone he could trust."

"*Thought* he could trust," Michaels corrected.

"Semantics. He wanted to go to the cops. Just come clean about everything like he forgot that eight billion dollars was on the line. Not a million. Not ten million. Eight *billion* dollars. I couldn't let him do that. I'm trying to put my life together, not trying to scatter what's left of the pieces."

Michaels shook his head.

"The money means that much to you? There are four deaths associated with this. "

"Four *explainable* deaths. Zeke caught you digging up his daughter's body and you killed him with a syringe stolen from my bag to frame your old friend, the doctor. You were so overwrought with guilt regarding the death of his daughter, you committed suicide. An accident, two suicides, a murder. By the time the smoke clears from this sleepy town, I'll be eight billion dollars richer on an island with no extradition."

"What happened to you, Ted? When did you become so damaged?"

"The moment Farnsworth got us all together. But that's okay, Bernie. I'll have the rest of my life to get over it…"

He raised the gun and pressed it against Michaels' head.

"But you won't," Strickler said.

Strickler barely got the words out before Michaels tossed the remaining dirt in his hand at Strickler's face. The initial flinch was all Michaels needed to get to his feet and take off running. Strickler pulled the trigger once, firing in Michaels' direction. The bullet grazed Michaels' neck, burning across it, creating a furrow in the skin. Michaels clutched the side of his neck with one hand as he crouched low among the headstones, putting distance between him and Strickler.

"Come on, Bern," Strickler shouted. "Give it up. Let's face it. You want to die. Your life is shit. Why prolong the inevitable?"

Strickler scanned the dark and the mist for any movement, ears focused to pick up any sound. He cut down a row of graves toward the back of the cemetery.

*****

Michaels did his best to keep low, but the effort made the wound in his neck bleed more. His eyes darted around. He had lost Strickler in the fog. He touched his neck and grimaced. His fingers were covered in blood, but he couldn't tell how bad it was. He fumbled his pockets for something to daub the wound. He found a used tissue and a half-crushed pack of cigarettes.

God, he wanted a smoke right now. He put one in his mouth for the taste and blotted his wound with the snot-rag. A nearby noise distracted him, and he left quickly, accidentally dropping the tissue as he moved into another, hopefully safer, location.

*****

Strickler advanced slowly, keeping the gun pointed forward ensuring that the deadly buffer was set between him and anything outside his reach. He noticed something on the ground and paused to inspect it. It was Michaels' discarded tissue, the blood still wet on his fingertips. He thought he had hit Michaels with the shot. Now confirmed, he didn't know how bad it was. One thing was sure – Michaels was close. The excitement made Strickler's heart skip a beat. One more murder was nothing at this point. He was all in.

Strickler kept his focus on tracking his friend, hoping that he'd find more discards that would bring him that much closer to his prey.

*****

Michaels knelt by a large headstone carved into the shape of a tree stump. He was so tired. He sucked on the unlit cigarette trying to draw whatever nicotine he could get. Everyone, even Strickler for that matter, was always telling him that smoking would kill him one day. How wrong they were, he thought.

He paused suddenly, taking the cigarette out of his mouth. An idea formed and bloomed and took root in his thoughts. Michaels wiped his neck with his hand and laid it across the stone. He wanted Ted to take notice. He wanted Ted to follow.

Michaels pressed on, only purposefully less quiet than before.

*****

Strickler came upon the blood on the tree stump headstone. He found something else on the ground – a full cigarette. He smiled at the find. Some habits die hard for people, he thought. It was an expression that had a keen applicability in the present.

Strickler's eyes surveyed the surrounding area. A sound close by got his attention. He raised his gun and shot in its direction. The bullet ricocheted off something metal and made a high-pitched *ping*! More noise gave away his prey's location. Michaels was getting desperate, Strickler thought. He was losing blood and he was desperate. It was time to put him down. Strickler eagerly picked up the pace.

*****

Michaels reached the far end of the cemetery out of breath. In front of him a large gravedigger's shack stood in poor condition. Side boards had popped loose, and part of the roof sagged where some of the roof beams had rotted. Michaels hobbled to the door and tested the handle. It wasn't locked, and he went inside.

The interior was larger than it appeared from the outside. There were rakes, shovels, a riding lawn mower, scythes, an assortment of carpentry tools, and cut marble headstones. In the back were two rooms – one with a cot and shelving, the other a makeshift kitchen with hotplates and bottled water. Michaels made his way to the farthest room in the back of the shed and sat down beneath a window. He took out his cigarettes. There was one left. He removed the lighter from his front pocket. How fitting he thought, a last cigarette before an execution.

He was two drags in when he heard Strickler outside. He got to his feet and peered out the window in time to see Strickler walking around the structure.

This was it, he thought as he inhaled deeply, then he sat back down with his back against the wall and just waited.

*****

A hard ten minutes passed before Strickler appeared at the shack. He had carefully followed the blood trail to this dilapidated structure. He didn't immediately go inside; instead, he watched and waited to make sure that Michaels was in the building. A brief surveillance of the shed confirmed that the door provided the only entrance, and the only exit. One window in the back provided a vent to filter in cool air. Michaels was cornered. The game was about to end.

He snuck quietly up to the front door. He touched the blood that had dropped on the rusted door handle and smiled. Blood was flowing freely; Michaels was hurt badly.

Instead of going in stealthily, Strickler pounded the front door with the butt of the gun.

"Bernie! Hey, Bernie! Gunshot wound? Where did I hit you, Bernie? The arm? The shoulder? Awfully painful, gunshots. Then when coupled with blood loss, well, that's just painful. It must be killing you."

He threw open the front door, gun out in front and ready.

There was no electricity. Strickler frowned and wrinkled his nose. Everything smelled like old manure. But one distinct odor came through, cutting through the agriculture – cigarette smoke. Strickler smiled as he moved cautiously deeper into the interior, moving the gun in every direction that he looked.

The final search of the last two rooms did not reveal Michaels. Strickler stared at the open window and the small step stool he assumed that Michaels had used to climb out. Blood on windowsill helped confirm Strickler's suspicions that Michaels somehow slipped out without making too much noise.

"Dammit," Strickler swore.

He turned and stormed back to the front door. He had to keep the pressure on Michaels. He couldn't risk having him get out alive from this cemetery and go running to that lawyer and confessing. Strickler estimated that the gunshot wound coupled with the blood loss would make Michaels move slowly. He'd be about twenty yards from the shed by the time Stricker caught up with him.

Strickler concentrated so hard on where he was going to shoot Michaels that he paid little attention to what was around him. He barely cleared the back rooms when –

WHAM!

Michaels slammed a pick handle against the arm that held the gun. The gun went flying. Strickler screamed in pain. The arm wasn't broken but it was severely fractured. Before Strickler recovered, Michaels leveraged the serendipity of the moment, and committed to an all-out assault.

Adrenaline-fueled, Michaels swung frantically. While his furious punches collided against Strickler's sides and shoulders in an act of self-preservation, they lacked the vigor to inflict the necessary punishment.

Strickler did his best to shield himself with his one good arm. He rolled with the punches, minimizing their force and making less of a target.

The writhing achieved its objective. The more Michaels' attacks were mitigated, the more desperate he felt and the wilder and uncontrollable his punches became. One of his swings hit a support beam, snapping Michaels' wrist like a twig. His loud scream resembled the hopeless wail of an animal once the jaws of a trap close around him.

Assuming his advantage, Strickler bum-rushed Michaels, sending the heavier man flying onto his back. He landed with a hard smack, his head bouncing off the wooden floor.

He kicked the downed man hard in the ribs, causing Michaels to turn back and forth. Unlike Strickler, Michaels body was less fluid in evading the onslaught. Instead of deflecting the blows to ride out their velocity, he turned into them, absorbing their force.

Between the blows and loss of blood, Michaels' strength steadily waned. His guard steadily dropped, allowing the attacks better access to vital organ areas, a vulnerability Strickler immediately recognized and exploited.

When it looked like he had complete control of the situation, Strickler paused his onslaught, breathing heavily, winded from his physical exertion. With his good hand, he grabbed Michaels by the shirt and brought him to his face. His wild eyes looked at the bloody mess of his friend. Cuts had opened on Michaels' cheek under his eye and along his right temple.

"Don't worry, Bern'. I'm not a complete son-of-a-bitch. I'll make sure your wife collects your life insurance."

He dropped Michaels back on the floor and grabbed a hand-held scythe from the wall.

Michaels barely moved. He had little energy left. His body ached, and his muscles were just too fatigued and old to put up any more of a fight. There, in his final moments on earth, he took the time to reflect on the errors of his life. What he would give for one chance to set the scales right. He wished he would have walked away from Farnsworth that night when he brought them all together into a permanent alliance of dependence. He wished he hadn't seen Alison Boyle that night and convinced his friends to follow her into the cemetery. He wished he had one chance to reverse the course of action that felled the dominoes that followed and brought him to this point.

He wished he had one final chance left for atonement.

Strickler tested the blade against the back of the thumb on his good hand. It wasn't as sharp as he had hoped, but coupled with the vicious point on the end, would adequately serve its intended purpose.

"Ted," Michaels said in a raspy voice.

Michaels waved him over. Strickler sighed.

"No last words, Bernie. Just die."

But like any bully that relished his position over the weak, Strickler allowed himself to enjoy the moment a beat too long. And it was in this false sense of gloating victory that Michaels saw and seized upon the one chance he sought.

He brought his foot up swiftly, the toe of his shoe digging hard into Stricker's scrotum.

The air immediately evacuated the doctor's lungs. Strickler felt the pain grab his lower intestines and not let go. His lower stomach tightened and throbbed as he saw stars. Michaels kicked him twice more on the spot before using the same foot to send the doctor sprawling across the floor.

Unfortunately for Michaels, Strickler landed near the gun on the floor. The two men looked at the .38, and then at each other. An unspoken confirmation passed between them that this fight was going to reach a conclusion, one way or another.

The two men moved simultaneously.

Desperation drove Michaels, a necessary jump-start that blunted the sharpness of the cracked ribs that he had just received. Gritting his teeth, he struggled to his feet as Strickler's hand grabbed the gun butt.

He only had two seconds. One to think and one to commit.

Run or fight, Bernie, he thought. *What's it going to be?*

The Bernie in college, the unmotivated slacker under the influence of Mexico-grown cannabis would have surrendered himself to the mercy of his attacker.

But not the guy about to charge the man pointing a gun at him.

Michaels' legs propelled him forward as he assumed the offensive. Survival meant closing the distance between them and negating the advantage of the .38.

Strickler fired as Michaels collided into him. The bullet ripped into his shoulder, significantly slowing his momentum. But not before he knocked the doctor backwards.

As he stumbled backwards, Strickler fired one more bullet into the tin roof, his one good arm desperately pinwheeling to keep him on his feet. His right foot caught the wheel of a grass seed spreader, altering his trajectory away from the wall and into an area reserved for unused headstones.

Strickler's head walloped a granite stone that had been carved to resemble a log fire, its sharp flames clawing upward. These penetrated the back of his skull and making a sickeningly impaling sound.

Strickler's face registered shock more than horror, frozen in a death scream that never sounded. Blood pooled steadily around the granite base.

Michaels clutched his left shoulder. He walked over and picked up the gun. Then he inspected the body of his friend. There was no breathing, no light in the doctor's eyes. He was dead. As dead as Farnsworth and Chance.

As dead as Alison Boyle.

Michaels picked up the .38 revolver and made his way out of the shack. He paused, resting against the door frame before he weaved his way back toward the Alison's grave. As he plodded forwarded, he gazed up at the night sky. Some of the fog had dissipated, finally allowing the brilliance of the stars to shine its light down on the cemetery. Despite the tragic events that had since ensued, Michaels could not help but think of the time Farnsworth got the group together for the first time.

Michaels was the last to be inducted into the fold. They had all been at an off-campus party, an around-the-world spectacle where every apartment in the building offered a drink from a specific country. Michaels was there to collect money owed to him for ten joints but had been pushed aside by his customer, the host of the party, and the four football player friends he had to ensure he didn't have to pay for the product.

They escorted Michaels out of the building, throwing him on the grass out front like garbage bags on trash day. About to chalk it up as an economic loss, he looked up and saw Farnsworth offering him a hand up. Chance and Strickler stood on either side of him like faithful bookends. He knew Strickler previously, but Chance was a relatively new face. Farnsworth asked if Michaels was all right. He also asked Michaels if he wanted him to get his money.

Farnsworth wasn't afraid of people just because they were bigger and stronger than he was. He wasn't scared of anything. And having that lack of fear gave him a mythical aura that few could understand, but everyone could appreciate.

Michaels tried to stop Farnsworth from going inside into the lion's den, but Chance held him back. He'd see, Chance told him. Farnsworth would make everything right.

Thirty minutes passed before they saw Farnsworth again, with the customer in tow behind him. Not only did he pay Michaels, but he apologized to him, promising never to repeat that lack of judgment again.

Michaels turned to Farnsworth. He didn't know what to say.

I'm Farnsworth, he said. And he held out his hand. They shook, and then Farnsworth introduced him to the others. He didn't know it then, but he understood it now. Each handshake was more than an introduction; it was a commitment. It was a pledge.

The men's friendship officially started that night.

And now, with the death of Stricker, that friendship officially ended this night.

Michaels stood over Alison's open grave, father and daughter united in the cold ground. Calm was the best way to describe how Michaels felt. His wounds throbbed but they were minor compared to what he was thinking and what he was emotionally feeling. He stood motionless for what seemed like an eternity, when it was only a few minutes. The words he said next seemed trite, but there were the most honest ones he had spoken in a very long time.

"I'm sorry, Alison," he said.

*****

Michaels' figure could easily be seen from Quinlan's vantage point on the ridge overlooking the cemetery. Michaels did not know he was there, but the lawyer had watched the whole scene play out, from the moment Strickler and Michaels first found the unmarked grave, to Zeke's interruption and subsequent murder, to the final mad-dash to see who would stand alone when the dust cleared. He had to hand it to Michaels; if Quinlan was a betting man he would have invested a substantial wager on Strickler emerging on top.

Tonight's course of events had unfolded favorably. Nothing went exactly to plan, and Quinlan was always concerned that the men would interact with townsfolk that were not on the payroll. That said, the hiccups were minimal, and despite a delay or two, they had figured out the last piece of the puzzle and found the right grave.

He was impressed with Farnsworth's methodical planning and his acute understanding of what the men would do and how they would react to certain stimuli. The gun and the drugs worked like a charm, achieving their intended effect of increasing distrust and sowing further doubt in the men about themselves, as well as each other. The more confronted with the very past they had tried so hard to forget, the more fractured they became, and like most paranoid shut-ins, they retreated into themselves wary of the motivations of outsiders.

Chance was the wild card. That was an unexpected turn of events that ultimately fell in Farnsworth's favor.

Per Farnsworth's direction, he fully expected that one or more of the men would "guess" the subject of the game prior to its conclusion. That was an immaterial consequence that bore no relation to the true intent of the game. Their implication in Alison's death and the opportunity to confront the men responsible for it was true attrition, the penance that had escaped the men for forty years. Eight billion dollars was worth the wringer that he had set up.

Michaels' voice carried enough for Quinlan to know that he was speaking, but not loud enough for him to hear his words. He was addressing the grave, the personification of a girl whose only crime was being in the wrong place at the wrong time.

Quinlan watched Michael's silhouette raise something to his head. The lawyer smiled. Farnsworth fully expected that whomever prevailed would be met with the consciousness of his own guilt. And with that weighing down on him, to fully embrace the only real course of action worthy of the game's conclusion.

*****

The gun's barrel was still warm from the previously fired shots. Michaels thought it was a comfortable feeling. Given everything that happened over the past few days, this was the most at peace Michaels had felt in a long time. How different life would have been if he had chosen a different school or different friends. If he had studied instead of smoked pot. If he had never met Farnsworth, or Chance, or Strickler.

If he had never crossed paths with a girl named Alison Boyle.

Murder wasn't just about the taking of a life; it was about remembering what you did. Not just once. But each and every day.

The shot was solitary. It sounded more like the pop of a packing wrap bubble than from a weapon. But it did the job.

*****

Quinlan watched Michaels' body fall to the ground in front of the grave. This town would have its fair share of problems when the sun came up. There would be police and the number of bodies would garner the attention of local and state news and probably make it on all the cable news channels. Reporters would dig for information and establish the friends' relationship to one another. The better ones would link their college to the one where one of the local's daughters had attended briefly before her untimely death. And the really good ones would make speculations and draw conclusions about the deaths of four men in connection to the girl's father on whose property they were residing for a weekend getaway. Whether they reported on part or the whole story, Alison Boyle's name would be resurrected, respected, and properly buried. There would be endless questions. That was okay. It was the price of doing business. Quinlan was prepared for the questions. Farnsworth had taken care of that.

The light dimmed, and Quinlan looked up at the sky. A new pack of clouds had rolled in, blanketing the moon in its thick folds save for one place where a lone star poked through. It was this star upon which Quinlan paused and reported the final update to his employer.

"It's finished, Neal," said Quinlan before turning and walking back toward his car.

9 781949 472158